FOREVERMORE

A NOVELLA BY
S. JEAN

ALSO BY S. JEAN

Hymn of Memory
The Devil in the Woods
Born of Scourge

~

FOREVERMORE

S. JEAN

For those of us with
tragedies in our hearts.

~

Content Warning

This is a story of necromancy and skeletons and as such, dead bodies and gore are to be expected. Also within are sexually suggestive scenes, abusive mentor relationships, and the devouring of hearts.
Read with care!

ONE

Delicate

BIRDS WERE DELICATE, THEIR BONES EVEN MORE SO. Too much magic and they would crack, turning to dust, and never again would fly across the breeze. This tiny thing was splayed on a plate made from lapis lazuli, each bone accounted for and arranged in such a way, its once wings were spread to remind it of the days it flew upon the air. That was the trick, after all; when the bones remembered the life they once had, magic takes to the hollow holes left behind and fills it with the desire to move again. Knowing how much magic, however, was tricky. Animals were easy in the grand scheme of the spell, at least. Their lives were once based on desire and instinct, making them altogether simple.

Humans were another matter entirely.

Nezael hadn't quite tried a human skeleton just yet; not for lack of wanting, however. His lord simply told him it wasn't time yet and the most Nezael had done was assist the process. Before he tried his own, he had to prove proficiency in simpler animals. And so, today was a test to see how he'd do with one of the most fragile sets of bones: the innerworkings of a bird.

His lord and master, the Great Sorcerer Carrow of the Thorns, watched Nezael work, standing behind him as a statue never once blinking as though to make sure he caught everything Nezael did (and didn't) do. It took everything Nezael had to focus on the bird and not the potential failure or success.

Taking a deep breath, he let the magic coil inside of him and pressed a gentle finger against the delicate bone that once made the wings. Mouthing ancient spells Carrow had penned himself, Nezael's magic flitted through his veins as though called. The bird's wings needed more magic than the rest of the body because the feathers no longer existed. Which, honestly, was a shame. The bird had once proudly displayed a vibrant red plumage and Nezael hated he'd had to peel the feathers and skin back to carefully extract the bones from within.

Just as well. With winter so soon, the bird wouldn't have survived. It was too late for it to join its brethren in migrating, having lulled itself into a false sense of security at Nezael's windowsill because of the crumbs he'd left for it. All he'd wanted was to listen to its song while studying; he hadn't meant to doom it. The poor thing relied on him instead of its own instincts and now it lay here on the slab. Perhaps its un-life would fare better...

Magic twitched and frayed against the distraction and Nezael clenched his jaw. *Focus*, he told himself.

At his coaxing, the magic stabilized and followed his finger. It threaded itself as a vibrant light cocooning itself around the bones to recreate the once muscle and tissue of the wing. It became a web of shimmering lines until it drew too soft and translucent for the naked eye to see. All it took for a sorcerer like Nezael and his lord, however, was a little more focus, and he saw past the reality of the bones and to the glimmering feathers he gently fashioned from the dormant magic threads. Without them, the skeleton bird simply wouldn't fly. Each time he finished a feather, he wove it into the unseen muscles and moved onto the next. Very soon, he had brought his finger across the entire body and all the way to the other wing. He sat back in his chair and gazed at his work in its entirety.

Currently, all the threads were slack against the bones, appearing almost like a shroud, but as far as he could see and quantify, it was all interwoven. Moment of truth. He looped careful fingers underneath the unseen threads and pulled them taut toward the core of the bird. The bones shuddered, rattling against the lapis, but remained whole. Good start. Nezael breathed in, gathering what magic lingered in the air, and gently blew a soft breath over the bones.

It took away any bit of magic not yet settled and what was settled, the breath sealed it within the hollow bones. He withdrew his hands, letting the magic go, and waited. At first, he thought he'd tightened all the spells too quickly and it failed to catch, but then the bird was up on its legs, shaking feathers no longer there. The motion made the bones rattle, disconcerting to those not used to it, but to Nezael, music. The bird even *chirped*, a sound made from the vibration of magic against the bones, and it trilled its usual soft song for him.

Nezael's lips stretched into a smile and he offered his finger to the bird like he had so many mornings before. On instinct with memory woven into the bones, the bird hopped up like it always did and gently pecked his hand, searching for stray crumbs.

Lord Carrow exhaled behind him, reminding Nezael he was there, and the tension stole out of the room with the breath. Two hands gently combed Nezael's feathery black hair from his forehead and Nezael followed the motion, tilting his head back. Carrow's hands were warm today, tingling with latent magic. He pressed a kiss to Nezael's forehead and his lips were just as warm.

"What did I tell you?" Carrow murmured, his voice its usual rumble deep in his throat. One of his hands trailed down Nezael's neck, its soft touch tempting Nezael to shiver, but he kept his composure. As Carrow rested his fingers against Nezael's collarbone, he offered his other hand to the bird. It happily hopped from Nezael's finger to Carrow's and he drew it closer.

"Talent and potential. Your worries were unfounded, my blossom." He smiled, his amber eyes twinkling with magic, and the bird took its first flight through the great hall. It flew up to the rafters and settled happily beside the skeletal corvid Carrow had raised long ago to act as his eyes outside the tower.

They both watched the bird go until it was settled in and once it was, Carrow gazed down at Nezael again. "You should have more confidence." His fingers gently pressed into Nezael's neck.

"I shall endeavor to be so," Nezael said, letting his lord feel his throat as he spoke. Another test. Magic carried across the body when cast and though Nezael knew he had dispelled it from his own fingers, many sorcerers forgot to let it go from their voice as well. If not released, the magic could continue unregulated through speech alone and form a mind of its own. "All of my success today has been because of you, my Lord, so it is only apt I thank you for this and more."

"Mm." Carrow released him. "You've done exceptionally well this year." He swept to Nezael's side to lean on the ritual slab they'd been using as a desk and allowed Nezael to stand. His eyes tracked Nezael's every move and Nezael studied him the same.

His lord was a tall man with broad shoulders and long elegant limbs which Nezael could have watched for days as they weaved magic. Never a movement out of place; he truly deserved the title of Great Sorcerer. Always dressed in the finest clothes one could weave on magic alone with protective enchantments imbedded into the fabric. Today, he wore his smokey gray coat with fur lining the inside with his usual black tunic, breeches, and boots spelled to glide on air if he wished when he walked. The coat was trimmed in glimmering gold that hid all manner of counter spells within. Not a seam was out of place. The muted colors never distracted from his eyes shining like ambers and from his vibrant honey brown waves he kept brushed back so it trickled down around his neck.

Nezael wasn't quite as perfect or finely put together

as his lord. While Carrow was tall and commanded a room on presence alone, Nezael was of middling height and a shrinking violet in comparison. He'd stopped growing a head shorter than his lord and wouldn't bulk up with weight despite attempts otherwise. Carrow had once said sometimes magic was the culprit. Given how young Nezael had been when he began weaving his own spells, it likely curbed much of his growth to further augment his magic instead. Although Carrow never expressed regret over this because steeping Nezael in magic while he was young made him worthy to be the apprentice he was trained to be.

In contrast to his lord's honey brown locks, Nezael's hair was a soft black with texture that reminded him of feathers. His eyes were softer than Carrow's sharp stare and were a subdued cherry compared to the brilliance of his amber. He wore simple tunics and breeches from town, not yet been given his own garments woven from magic. Maybe soon, when Carrow felt Nezael was a true necromancer like him.

It had to be soon given the way Carrow gazed at him with all the hunger of having an eager student and all the delight in the world of that said student having passed one of the most fragile tests.

Nezael couldn't help the pride swelling in his chest. It must have shown. Carrow's eyes darted to his and Nezael forced himself to keep eye contact. "Yes, my Lord?"

Carrow shook his head, his smile so warm and inviting, Nezael could have stared at it all day to memorize it for as long as he could. "Oh, naught is amiss, my blossom." Carrow reached out and cupped Nezael's face in his hands. "Isabella wanted your assistance once you were done in here. I have meetings to attend with visitors coming in, so do right by her and please, stay out of sight, hm?"

"Of course." Nezael smiled and his whole body warmed when Carrow pressed his lips to Nezael's forehead again. "Are many coming this time?"

"Enough to keep me wary." He dropped his hands and stepped away. "Perhaps soon we'll be able to do more than simply hide. See to Isabella now. I must prepare."

Carrow headed out of the hall without another warm word and the corvid took flight after him. The creature was a magical marvel on its own; Carrow could see through its eyes and even control its movements if he wanted to. Nezael had a lot more to learn before he could even think to try that. He peered up at his own tiny bird. It had nestled itself against the crook in the rafters, looking right at home.

"Stay wherever you wish," he said gently. The bird cocked its head toward him. "My home is yours forevermore." He blew it a gentle kiss, letting magic carry the gesture farther, and was delighted when the bird shuffled unseen feathers in reply.

Hopefully, it felt as at home as Nezael did and he trekked after his lord.

Nezael didn't know how long he'd been at the tower—or even his own age, if he was honest—but it had been his home for as long as he could remember. There were snapshots of a life before the tower, but they were silent and fuzzy with nothing to say about them but vague shapes and ideas. Nezael ignored them. What did the past matter when he was here now? With a Lord who smiled at him so? With magic thrumming through his body, wanting to help the world change? And who could grant him the ability but his one and only lord?

As such, this tower hidden past the forest full of brambles and thorns was his home. Stone walls fortified with latent magic, windows which creaked when opened (if they even could be), and drafts aplenty ghosted through hallways covered in mismatched tapestries to stave off the long winters. Rugs of all kinds covered the floors, each one treaded on for years before and would still be around years later, creating a splash of muted colors across the halls. Lord Carrow never quite made the place homey—he likely hadn't intended to spend so long here—but Nezael had done his best to bring life to it once he saw how the town south past the brambles looked.

There, the interiors were warm, with golden hues from the windows always lighting the rich warmth of the wood. Colors aplenty were draped across barren walls in patterned fabrics and Nezael loved it all. It reminded him of life and he wanted it here too. Sure, his attempts were paltry at best, relying on what little he received from selling potions in the marketplace during the summer, but it let him enjoy the tower more. He'd even hung bushels of dried flowers from the wooden beams, their muted shades the perfect pop of color most hallways needed, and bought old and worn tapestries from merchants to give it second life on their walls. This way, they had colors among the cold drafty hallways. Though his lord never quite complimented the frivolous change, Nezael had caught him smiling at everything more than once.

Nezael turned into the spiral stairwell leading to Isabella's workroom. It was located in the lowest room the tower had to offer so that if one of her potions met an unfortunate end, the rest of the tower would be spared.

Isabella had agreed with adding more colors to the tower so much, that she'd decked out her workroom in all the shades she could gather. Bright, gaudy cloth that never seemed to dull went across any wall she wasn't using. Those that weren't covered had honeycomb shaped shelves made of wood fixed to them, the wood made of soft, golden shades. Each cubby was filled with jars housing all manner and color of herbs. The center of the room contained her table with a cauldron and burner, various glass measuring instruments, stone pestles, and even her bronze scales. The floor was covered in rugs crisscrossing on top of one another, each one soft on her skeletal feet. Her bed was pushed into one corner, draped in as many colors as the floor and walls, and she'd hung up a floral printed tapestry to act as canopy over her bed. All the pops of colors were dear to Isabella, what she called memories of her excursions to the town marketplace with Nezael by her side.

Isabella herself was dressed in thick fabrics as vibrant as her personality. She always kept a shawl wrapped around her head to protect her polished skull, tucking it in expertly every time, and wore long robes to hide the fragility of her bones within. She wrapped her skeletal fingers in strips of fabric that differed in color from one finger to the next and on top of that, she wore jeweled rings enchanted to protect her hands. Nezael didn't know how old she was (and he learned very quickly it was a rude question) and had no idea how long she'd been Lord Carrow's skeletal potions master, but Carrow's magic within her bones was as strong as ever, woven so precisely, it was as though she still maintained the fluidity of her once muscles.

She looked up from her measuring beaker as Nezael slipped past the curtain in the doorway. The room always had an air of incense and herbs Isabella herself could no longer smell, but to Nezael, it smelled like home.

Though Isabella had no face, as was the case of all the raised skeletons, Nezael still felt the warmth of a smile as she gazed at him.

"I see you're about and smiling," she said, her voice oscillating against the magic in her skull. She never knew if it was really how her voice had sounded in life, but Nezael liked it for what it was. It had a strange kind of cadence he adored. "To what do I owe the pleasure of this smile, my little lord?"

Nezael came up to her table and let the smile stretch. "I raised the bird! None of the bones cracked once and I really did it this time."

Bones pushed against Nezael's leg and he glanced down. The cat he had raised earlier this year rubbed against him like it always did when he visited Isabella. He gently bent down and massaged its forehead with his finger. A glint of magic reacted, reinvigorating the cat, and it sauntered back to the bed where it must have been napping before he came in.

Isabella clapped her hands. "I knew it was only a matter of time before you mastered a bird! Our Lord must have been *so* ecstatic. Why, that must have been him I heard dancing across the floor above."

Sarcasm dripped from her voice and Nezael bit back his snicker. Lord Carrow was indeed hard to impress and held many of his emotions close to his chest.

"He was happy," Nezael said and left it at that as the ghost of the kiss fluttered across his skin. "As much as he's ever happy, I suppose. He told me you needed my help?"

Isabella paused, tilting her head like she was confused, and then chuckled. "Oh dear. I was fussing and he must have heard me. Well, a bored little lord such as thee needs distractions, I suppose." She set her beaker down and shuffled past him, the aroma of spice and herbs trailing in her wake as it cascaded off her robes, and he followed her to the honeycomb shelves. She trailed a boney finger across the contents until she found the jar she searched for and wiggled it free.

Empty, but the lingering magic inside from the herbs that once was made the glass shimmer. Nezael took it and read the label. "Vistarium herbs?"

"Yes, they grow very precariously and are even more precarious to gather." Isabella returned to her table and pulled a tome of herbs out from her pile of books. She never quite treated her books with the same reverence as her herbs, but then again, she likely had all the pages memorized. This was purely for Nezael's benefit.

She flipped through the thick vellum pages until she reached the center. On one side of the spread, there was a carefully rendered sketch of the plant and herb in question, and on the other, the list of potions to be made with such a plant.

"It absorbs magic," Isabella explained, too impatient to wait for Nezael to read the entire thing. "Given how late it is in the year, it's risky for me to search for the plant on my own. It'd take what scant power I have left." Without magic, skeletons ceased being able to move. Dangerous for her when her magic was at its thinnest so close to winter. "All our wards use these herbs as a base to protect us from any strange spells used against us and our lord has been going through it like it's going out of style." She tilted her head toward Nezael in what he construed as a mischievous grin. "You up for fetching me some more? I do know how you adore walks outside."

Even if sometimes Lord Carrow wished Nezael never left at all. Nezael smiled all the same and nodded. "Of course." He giggled as Isabella leaned forward and bumped her bony cheek against his. Her magic tickled across his skin, reminding him of a kiss on the cheek, and she withdrew to gather supplies for him.

Normally, she'd accompany him on forest excursions and sometimes to the marketplace in town, but given Carrow was meeting with others today, she probably had her hands full on a truth serum to keep their guests truthful. It was simmering in her cauldron if Nezael had to guess; it always smelled like roses. There were too many who wanted their lord dead, so the serum was a requirement.

Nezael didn't mind heading out alone. Once Isabella had given him basic information for finding the herb (it made magic thin when it grew and she described how the petals were a golden yellow in bloom) and saddled him with a cloth bag and jar, he was back up the stairs to get dressed for the trek. If it was summer, he would have gone as he was—loose tunic and leggings, even foregone shoes completely—but it was closing in on winter and he needed more layering than that.

On went the thicker tunic, the cloak lined in dark fur, his thicker leather boots, and he remembered his dagger. Usually used for rituals, but it came in handy for cutting herbs and also protection. Although he hadn't had to protect himself. Yet. His lord always reminded him to be careful and having it was surely better than not.

Nezael headed out into the noon sunshine and peered up at his home. Their tower was a solid brick and stone building hidden in the middle of the woods. It was the color of a tree's bark, the bricks light and dark with wards hidden within, and the windows absorbed the sunlight instead of reflecting it. Vines slithered up the front and, in the spring and summer, blossomed so many different flowers Isabella collected for potions. Now, they were withered and dormant. Instead, what bloomed now was a line of razor-sharp bushes across the front gardens. Always gave late autumn flowers which fell off and was collected at the first snowfall. Past them were walls constructed to protect the tower within should anyone attempt to invade. It made the place a kind of sanctum, in a way.

Magic was warm in the walls, each one carefully warded, and as Nezael passed each one, the power grew weaker and weaker until he'd stepped outside the spells altogether.

It was always a shock to the system. Once suddenly so invited and warm, only to be deposited in the cold and the sudden realization he was alone. Looking back, one would hardly guess the tower was there at all. It was perfectly obscured beyond the trees, the brambles and thorns, and even the walls made it look like a ruin long since plundered. Safe in all regards in its bubble of protection.

Being out here, however, meant being away from that very same protection and Nezael tightened his focus. Though the forest this deep was seldom traveled, it did Nezael no good to walk as though entranced by a dream. Magic made the place grow too wild to tend safely, keeping the travelers at the path, but sometimes people wandered in. Those usually became skeletons under Carrow's lone will. Thankfully, it didn't happen often enough to arouse suspicion. Locals said the forest was haunted, so the only ones who did get caught were travelers no one would miss.

Though Nezael kept an eye out for danger, again and again he found himself relaxing simply being in the forest by himself. The leaves had changed to honey oranges and yellows with red splashed between them. The sun was vibrant today too, penetrating the foliage and sheathing the twisting footpaths in dappled light. Even the ground was aglow with changed leaves, creating a mosaic of colors Nezael would have happily shuffled through if he didn't have a job to do.

"Focus," he told himself quietly. "Vistarium herbs."

Over the years while assisting Isabella when she

scrounged up herbs, Nezael had learned one thing: herbs with magical properties hummed. It was a hard sound to parse in the chatter of the forest or even in the town if he had to go that far, but one of his lord's lessons had been to hone his ability to listen. He set his feet, held still, and closed his eyes to do so. Not to the soft chatter of animals scurrying as they prepared for the winter to come, not the soft coos of birds as they fluffed up their nests, but to the soft twinkle magic made against the threads of reality.

In places such as the forest, the magic ran through *everything* and made it somewhat difficult to sort through. Other places, like the town, were a little more barren, but magic lingered there too. Except if the herbs absorbed magic, he was searching for an absence. Silence.

The lack of any twinkle at all took him into the overgrown patches of grass and wildflowers and he kept his footsteps as light as possible to keep himself obscured. It led him across the forest and it was only when the sun was receding lower in the sky, making the shadows darker, did he come across the grove he was looking for. The magic inside was outright gone, making the whole place feel off.

Nothing stood out. The trees were bent protectively around the grove, long bare branches bending low as the muted reds and oranges covered the grass. Nestled at the base of those trees, however, were bushels of bright yellow petals. Actually, those were much brighter than they had any right to be this time of year and Nezael dug out the sketch Isabella had given him. There it was. Vibrant yellow petals soaking in magic to last through the winter. Supposedly was beautiful in bloom with snow dusted across it. In fact, according to Isabella's notes, right after the first snowfall was the perfect time to grab the herbs—they'd be at their peak then—but their lord needed the wards now and Nezael got to work.

Honestly, out of everything from Lord Carrow's teachings, Nezael liked foraging for herbs the most. He felt connected in a way he never had to the world around him. Life in the tower was isolating and it was easy to lose track of the days as a result. Out here, however? Gently folding branches back to find the correct bud within? Let him touch the world and be part of it in some fashion. He liked it. Maybe he should have been Isabella's apprentice instead.

As he searched and snipped, collecting the fallen buds in Isabella's jar, another sound began to echo through the grove. He ignored it at first, attributing it to nature being nature, but it continued long enough, it drew his attention. First came the woosh through the air, snapping against the magic past the grove, and then came the decided thud of steel cleaving wood in two. After a pause, the same sounds came again. Rhythmic, almost. Sometimes, between the sounds, was a husky hum lilting through the trees upon the air.

Curiosity got the better of Nezael—who in their right mind came this deep into the forest to simply chop wood?—and he ventured toward the sound. It led him gently around the bright yellow bushels, footsteps soft between fallen leaves, and he went from tree to tree to stay hidden. When Nezael was close enough he could taste the steel as it cut through the air, he pressed himself against the nearest tree and peered around it.

There was another clearing connected to a trail he'd never noticed before. A small wooden cabin had been built close to the dirt road and it looked neither new or old. Smoke billowed out of the stone chimney, but all the curtains were drawn across the windows. Nezael's gaze shot to the middle of the clearing where another thud made him jump. A rather large stump was there, only a few paces away, with a pile of firewood. Poised with an axe aloft was a tall man facing away from Nezael. Wide shoulders, sculpted muscles along his bare back, and his tawny skin glistened with sweat underneath the afternoon sun. Low-riding breeches hugged the shape of his legs and his leather boots looked well-traveled. Glimmering russet hair was gathered at the back of his head, leaving waves long enough to tumble down his neck.

Nezael watched, entranced as the axe came down and the way the man's muscles moved in tandem with the strike. If only he could trace them, memorize the way they moved for when he had to raise a human skeleton. Again and again, he watched the perfect arc the man made with his arms and how swiftly the axe came down so precisely. It was such a soothing rhythm, Nezael felt comfortable resting against the tree to keep watching.

The man must have been the woodsman for the town. There was more than enough firewood for one house in the pile and that wasn't even counting the bunches already twined together near the cabin. Maybe Nezael could make an excuse to get firewood from him. Simply to appease his scientific curiosity of the man's muscles, of course. As he thought of the ways to do so, the axe came down and was left in its groove in the stump. Before Nezael's thoughts caught up to why, the man had turned to gather the fallen pieces.

Their eyes met.

Nezael shoved himself behind the tree, pulse roaring in his ears, and just when he thought perhaps he'd been fast enough, his heel cracked a twig.

"Hello?" the man called, voice tense, and everything felt like it stilled around them. Nezael covered his mouth to smother his sudden panicked breathing. "Is... is someone there?" The man hesitated and then came the soft sounds of his approach.

Nezael's panic blinded him to all the spells he'd memorized to protect himself. He was never supposed to be seen and if so, deal with it so no one could say he was ever there and now here he was. Absolutely seen.

The man's footsteps were light and careful, not like someone who wanted to hurt him, but Nezael wasn't going to take that chance. He sucked in a breath and ran, uncaring about the racket he made through the brush. He knew the woods better than anyone; no one would find him so long as he got a head start.

There was a sudden burst of activity behind Nezael as soon as he ran, but he continued sprinting and didn't look back. Eventually, those noises ceased and it was only Nezael.

Not that he was going to stop running. Safety was the tower. He clutched his bag close, pressing the jar of definitely not enough herbs against his chest, and focused on keeping his legs moving. By the time he pushed himself into the bubble of protection around the tower, his legs wanted to give out beneath him. He let them, collapsing to his knees, and bent low to catch his breath. A few of the patrolling skeletons noticed him, but he waved them off. He was fine. No harm done.

Even if his heart hammered against his chest like a bird trying to escape.

Once he'd regained control of his breathing and managed to stand, he headed for the tower doors. He'd calmly tell Isabella he only found a few perfect buds and he'd go out again tomorrow. No need to alarm anyone that someone had built a cabin in a clearing just outside their wards. It wasn't like a simple woodsman would be a danger to them.

He was still piecing the story together in his head when he pushed the tower doors open and promptly ran into Bellamy, his lord's first skeleton and oldest friend. Bellamy was sturdy and surefooted with what Carrow had once called a dancer's frame, and he caught Nezael around the shoulders without so much as wavering. Like Carrow, Bellamy always dressed exquisitely, although he leaned toward the richer colors like the mauve and red jacket he wore now. It reminded Nezael of the bards he'd seen in the town square, but Bellamy adamantly refused to play any instrument.

"Oh, my little lord," he said, his voice with its usual velvety tenor. Nezael could have honestly listened to him talk all day. "What's wrong?" Bellamy gently touched Nezael's face, his bones cold. "Your face is flushed—"

"Nothing," Nezael said, breathless. "I promise."

Though Bellamy had no expressions, Nezael distinctly felt as though the skeleton gave him a suspicious look. With a shake of his head, Nezael pulled out the jar of admittedly too few herbs, and held it up. "Something was near the clearing I went to. I panicked. This is all I got. I'm sorry—I don't want to disturb our lord with such frivolities."

"Is that all?" Bellamy said. "Isabella will understand. What matters is that you were not harmed." He tilted Nezael's chin to look up at him. "Were you?"

"Just my pride," Nezael admitted.

Bellamy chuckled. "There is always tomorrow." He gently took the jar. "I'll tell Isabella to save you the teasing. You compose yourself in the library. You know how Carrow would fret if he saw how flushed you are. Study what he told you to."

The library was the only place he and his lord alone had access to. A sacred place where Nezael could relax by himself. He quickly nodded, understanding that Bellamy was trying to help. Bellamy squeezed his shoulder and headed off for Isabella's workroom, calling out for her in a teasing way, while Nezael hurried through the hall. He slowed down immediately, reminding himself he had no reason to panic inside the walls of the tower, and afforded himself a deep breath.

Voices drifted out from the great hall at the end of the main thoroughfare and Nezael hesitated before he drew closer. There were many at once, speaking over one another, and Carrow's sharp and quick voice answered them all. One peek couldn't hurt. Nezael pressed up to the door and peered through the crack Bellamy must have been spying through the same.

His lord stood at the ritual slab, the lapis plate gone and so too anything else they'd been using to raise the bird. His presence commanded the room of people Nezael had never seen before and nor did he wish to commit them to memory. Mercenaries and travelers were all they were. Nezael did, however, take note of those laying on the floor, eyes dull. The effects of the truth serum Isabella had prepared. One lie was all it took. A pity, but there'd be new skeletons in the coming day. His lord would shuffle the bones to confuse any soul lingering on so they'd become perfect soldiers unaware he'd been the reason for their deaths. Maybe Nezael would watch the process. Maybe even raise his own.

For now, he headed to the library as Bellamy suggested. Every wall was filled with books collected throughout the years, ones Carrow penned himself or won from other sorcerers, and all were helpful in some fashion or another. The only book Nezael wanted right now, however, was *his* spell book. The one with the personal touches of his own spells that he needed to keep safe. It was in the central fireplace, burning as an enchanted flame only he could touch. Best way to keep it hidden.

As Nezael reached in, the fire hummed across his skin like kisses and released him as he withdrew with his book. Holding it close, he flicked a hand at the fireplace to ignite a real fire and the logs within burned bright. The room was soon sheathed in renewed warmth and Nezael settled in on the couches nearest the fireplace.

Try as he might, however, he couldn't quite concentrate on studying. Endlessly, his thoughts drifted to the man in the clearing. The sculpt of his body. The way his muscles moved across his back in decided movements.

Even the soft way he'd spoken—the voice now sending a delightful shiver through Nezael's body—like he was afraid of spooking Nezael.

And yet, he had, and Nezael knew that he should have been frightened being seen at all, but a thrill moved through his body. It left behind a sensation that wasn't altogether uncomfortable. Nezael settled in, thinking of the man entirely, and forgot all about his spells.

TWO

ERRANDS

THE FOLLOWING MORNING, NEZAEL WAS ABLE TO swallow down breakfast before his lord came looking for answers, jar in hand. Carrow listened patiently as Nezael told his tale... well. Most of it. He avoided mentioning the woodsman outright and tried to blame his nerves on some silly forest creature spooking him, but Carrow wasn't altogether convinced that it was nothing.

"Protecting yourself is as easy as grasping the magic latent around you," Carrow explained after bringing Nezael back to the great hall. The bodies had been taken away and without the crowd, it was their magic room once more.

Carrow demonstrated weaving a spell with his hands and arms, sliding them across the magic in the room. Nezael watched the waves move in tandem with Carrow for a few passes before Nezael followed the motion with his own arms.

"You *can* use magic from within yourself," Carrow amended as he folded his arms behind his back to watch Nezael, "but you'll only endanger yourself that way by leaving yourself prone to exhaustion. Use what the elements freely provide. Air is plentiful. Bend it to your whim." When he was happy with Nezael's motions, he brought his arms back in front and snapped them through the air with purpose. Magic lightning burst across his fingertips and shot out, crackling through the air and into the wall.

It was done so quickly, Nezael jumped and then could only stare in awe.

Necromancy took magic from inside the caster because raising the dead required an exchange of energies. Since that was what Nezael was training to be, it was the only way he knew how to use magic. He'd never considered manipulating magic outside himself. Unfortunately, this took him a few tries. Any time his own magic came bubbling to the surface to aid him, Carrow caught his hands unafraid and told him to try again. Frustration threatened to undo the lesson entirely until finally, lightning struck from Nezael's own fingers. It had not the whipcrack of Carrow's own, however, but a rather weak spark. It still left its own mark on the wall at least, and from the look of pride on Carrow's face, Nezael could have sworn he'd done more.

"Better," Carrow said and gently drew his fingers through Nezael's hair. "No more being spooked. One day, you'll need to protect yourself as much as it pains me to admit." His hand drew downward until he'd cupped Nezael's cheek. "Do your errands, my blossom, and be back before it grows dark. We'll have more lessons after supper."

Nezael leaned into Carrow's hand before he took it back. "Will you not come with me?"

Carrow adjusted the lapels of his coat, a slight upturn of his lips in a smile. "If only I could afford a stroll in the forest. I must focus on our new skeletons. See to your own errands."

Nezael watched Carrow leave before he tried the spell once more. Alone, he let his own magic surface. It buzzed pleasantly through his veins and as it collected across his fingertips, and he whipped it toward the marks on the wall. The arc it made from his arm and outward unfurled all the way to the ceiling like white-hot ribbons before it struck true. The wall smoldered and Nezael smiled to himself. That would surely protect him, no matter what way he used the magic.

Even if it wasn't quite protection he desired.

~

ERRANDS MEANT HELPING THE SKELETONS IN WHATEVER they needed. Isabella, of course, wanted her herbs, insisting in the utmost importance getting them by tonight, but when Nezael collected his things, it was Agatha dragging him out of the tower for a quick market run before any herb scrounging. Agatha was the tower's cook even though she'd lost her sense of taste and smell when she became a skeleton. Unlike Isabella and Bellamy, she was raised after Nezael came to the tower. He'd helped clean her bones and had been a rapt audience when his lord did the necessary magic to raise her, but he'd been so young and it was so long ago now, he still couldn't grasp what all his lord had done specifically.

Agatha was a stout woman, half a head shorter than Nezael himself, but her presence was loud enough to fill the whole room. She hardly spoke about specifics in her life before she was raised, but she always had a story to tell about all her recipes and Nezael loved listening to them as she cooked. She always made sure Nezael tasted everything for her and frequently sneaked him desserts she baked late into the night.

Seen as they were headed into town, Agatha dressed in layers of robes to give the appearance of a squishy body beneath it all and had her skull hidden under her hood and scarves. She'd even added a pillow to her chest to, as she put it, give her the bosom she'd once had.

"I think that's what we miss most," she'd said as she'd stuffed the pillow into the robes, "the tangible pieces of ourselves we lost. Nothing magic can do will replicate what we once knew so well."

Thankfully, most people didn't look closely whenever Nezael ventured into town with a skeleton. It helped he looked as normal as could be. It was colder today too, the air biting more than it had yesterday, and everyone had cloaks and scarves obscuring any notable features. Agatha blended right in.

Nezael couldn't remember the town's name, but every week he would come down with one of the skeletons to get provisions for the tower. They never stayed long enough for anyone to recognize Nezael from previous weeks and though it was lonely, Nezael understood the need. Necromancy was a fringe magic art according to his lord, so it was best not to draw attention to themselves by dawdling around in the open. Summer meant selling potions, but the crowds were so thick then and sellers aplenty, no one bothered to memorize one seller over the other.

The town was built some time ago along the bank of the river sliding through the forest and as such, the entrance to town from the forest was across a wooden bridge. It had been decorated for the coming winter with dried holly plants fixed to the posts to ward off any lingering beast thinking to prowl into town. The paltry charm never worked on skeletons and Nezael doubted it would work if any beast really wanted into town. Even still, as he passed, he gently pushed a little magic into the holly buds to help.

Past the bridge, the road took them into the town's center where it looked like a place so far removed from the forest. Wooden buildings sat upon stone foundations, glass lamps lined a paved stone road, and there were so many paths snaking through town with more buildings all over. The center had a large fountain with benches around it and while sometimes, Nezael wished he could sit and simply watch people go by, he always had to refrain to not draw attention to himself. Dried flowers had been hung from the lamp posts, bringing pops of color to them, and some buildings had been decorated in pine garlands for the coming winter.

Further away from the town were farmlands, but they were already finished with their harvests. Most of it had already been culled and sold, but there were a few farmers in the market looking to offload anything they hadn't needed for coin. Agatha immediately honed in on them and with any luck, they'd have more than enough for Nezael through the winter.

Other sellers were open in various stalls and tents around the farmers and each one sold a variety of wares. From clothing, fabric, jewelry, magic charms—it was really anything anyone could sell to get rid of it before winter. Markets weren't open once the first snow fell, and it was only a matter of days before it happened.

As they went, Agatha happily filled her basket with items traded for coin and she hummed as she moved from stall to stall. Further down the street, Nezael noticed the bakery's doors open and caught the aroma of sugar in the air. Maybe he could convince her to fill up her pantries with little cakes so he had something sweet to eat this winter. Or at least something for the walk home.

"Come now, little lord," Agatha whispered as she drew him over to a bushel of crops for sale a farmer had twined together. "Don't go eyeing those sweets yet. You need more than that to last through the winter. Pick a bushel you like and I'll teach you how to cook them fore I sleep."

Every winter, Lord Carrow placed the skeletons into slumber. It was to help their bones not become brittle with the harsh temperatures. Slumbering also helped the magic latent in the tower strengthen them. The only skeleton ever left awake aside from a few patrolling ones was Bellamy. He was old enough his bones were calcified and hardy, years of magic wrapped around them.

And this year, Lord Carrow would be resting with his

skeletons. Nezael's stomach twisted thinking about it. In all his years at the tower, Nezael and Carrow had gone through the winters together using the private moments to study magic uninterrupted. Granted, being wholly alone with his lord sometimes was fraught with dealing with the way his temperament swung from day to day, but Bellamy was always there to help ground their lord.

With all of Carrow's plans coming to fruition finally—and they must have been because he was entertaining mercenaries of all people—he needed rest so he could gather his own magic. Beyond Bellamy, Nezael would be on his own to learn or not learn whatever he wanted through the winter. It was equal parts freeing, but also frightening. What if his lord awoke displeased with what he did or didn't do? What if—

"My little lord?" Agatha was looking at him, concern in her voice.

Nezael shook off his unease. "Yes. Um." He drew his gaze over the offered crops and had no idea what they even were. He pointed at the one with the tall stalks of green. "I think this one will be sufficient."

Agatha chuckled. "I'll leave Bellamy and you good instructions." She traded a handful of coins and took the bushel to string along her back. "Come, we should pick up some yarn so Bellamy has something to do. I'm sure he'd love to teach you to knit without our lord stealing you away to practice magic."

As Agatha fussed over yarn colors and spoke at length about it to the shopkeeper and others like they were old friends, Nezael remained outside and peered across the moving crowds. There was someone selling firewood not far from the craft shop and they were carefully twined together, just like the bundles the man from yesterday had at his cabin. Thinking of him at all sent a flutter up Nezael's body, making his cheeks warm, and he craned his neck to see if the man was even there.

Everyone blended together, faces unknown and bodies under cloaks and scarves. No one he recognized. He tried to not look disappointed as Agatha pulled herself free of the heated debate about yarn quality. She had another bag slung on her shoulder now, full of yarns of all color.

"Well, I've grabbed everything on my list." Agatha followed Nezael's gaze and patted his arm. "We've no need of firewood. Our lord has a skeleton to chop some of our own."

"Right," Nezael said and eyed Agatha. "No sweets this time?"

Agatha cackled, shaking her head. "I'm making you tarts later! Be patient."

That would taste better than anything they could buy at the bakery and Nezael smiled at her. She looped her arm into Nezael's and led him out of the market. Like the wind, they trickled out and no one would remember they were ever there.

They followed the usual trail alongside other leaving travelers and when Nezael felt a ward of his lord's nearby, he and Agatha pretended to rest and drink tea from her bag. Well, she mimed drinking it to not ruin her robes. It wasn't long before they were alone and slipped through the ward unseen. The paths were familiar here, surrounded by thorns and brambles while magic sung softly across the air in greeting. When they were within sight of the walls, Agatha slowed and extracted the jar of too few yellow buds from inside her cloak.

"Here," she said. "Go fetch Izzy her petals. I can make the walk back from here." She beckoned Nezael closer and he bent lower so she could bump her cheek to his. "I'll have sweets ready when you return."

He smiled at her, feeling the same expression radiate in return. "I'll be back soon."

"I'm roasting that hen for supper too! If you get lost, just follow all the good smells back." She wiggled his fingers at him and practically skipped back to their tower.

Alone, Nezael gazed along the path he'd taken to the grove. His stomach fluttered anew, thinking of seeing the woodsman again, and Nezael breathed out to settle his feelings. It was useless indulging the emotion (although he still secretly held it close) because it would and could not lead to anything other than a little glance. He'd get the herbs and then leave.

Retracing his steps from yesterday was easy and he followed the same trail. The sun was sallow today, not the bright golden it had been, and the skies had turned gray. The foliage above wasn't as brilliantly colored without the sun and the wind bit through them, crumbling them to pieces as it blew by. He drew his cloak tighter around himself and hurried.

The bushels were still their brilliant yellow in the grove when Nezael arrived and he got to work. The petals clipped off neatly with the edge of his knife and shivered as Nezael touched them. The numbing sensation of magic being taken was all too distracting against his bare fingers, but he persevered and trimmed as many herbs as he could. He continued until the jar was almost full and by then, his hands were frigid and red with no magic keeping them warm.

That was enough. He secured the jar in his bag and idly blew into his fingers to warm them up before heading back. Standing there, still and silent, he heard it. The log splitting from an axe cleaving it in two.

Without his intention, the same rhythmic sound entranced Nezael a second time.

He resisted, he really did, but his legs had other ideas and brought him right back to the tree from before and he afforded himself one quick look.

The woodsman was there yet again, woefully with a shirt on this time. Nezael's cheeks warmed, embarrassed that he was disappointed at all, and he tried to shake the shirtless image from his mind.

With the same deftness as before, the man struck the logs in two, only needing one good slice for each of them. Nezael had no idea *why* the motions were mesmerizing or why this simple man was so fascinating. Whatever it was, it made Nezael's stomach flutter in such a way he'd never felt before.

And this was where it ended. Nezael absolved to let himself have one more lingering look. Before he turned to lock it away in his memory, the man paused. Nezael once more wasn't fast enough to hide before the man peered his way. Their eyes met a second time, Nezael's entire body flipped into flight mode as his heart hammered in his chest, but then the man smiled.

The world seemed to stall and stutter. It was such a

gentle curve of his lips against the stubble lining his lower jaw. Something so infectious, Nezael's own lips wanted to mimic the motion.

"Hey," the man said, his voice sending a shiver down Nezael's back. "I didn't mean to scare you before." He gently put the axe down and faced Nezael slowly, like he feared frightening Nezael again.

No. He'd never been frightened. Not with what he could do with magic. He wanted to scoff at the idea, but he was frozen still. If he wasn't frightened, then what was this blasted emotion coiling around his heart for a man he didn't even know?

"My name's Yorick," the woodsman continued. "You don't quite look like a wood nymph—although you're certainly as fast as one."

Nymphs were magical creatures residing in woods across the land and were made up of magic. As far as Nezael knew, the woods had no nymphs of their own— his lord's magic would have driven out any hiding amongst the trees. There was a water nymph in the nearby lake upstream, however, but she kept to herself and Carrow never bothered her.

Focus. Nezael shook his head and bit back from engaging in conversation. "I should go," he said instead and let his legs take flight to dash away.

"Wait!"

It was silly. Dangerous. His lord didn't even know someone had built a cabin so close to his wards; it was too dangerous to be friendly and Nezael squashed the fluttering feelings down as his pulse raced. He wouldn't come back for some time—they had enough herbs now—maybe the winter would drive this man—*Yorick*—closer to town.

Except the same thought made Nezael sad.

The distraction masked the way the cold wind became suddenly colder and only when Nezael's cheek cracked from a needle-sharp gust did he pause. A glob of blood ran down to his jaw and he stopped outright, suddenly steeped back in reality. That was no ordinary wind. He pressed a hand to his cheek and peered upward, eyes wide.

There. It had moved behind him. He turned and found a ghostly form befitting a doe in the brush and he would have been tricked if he hadn't felt the magic tumbling off it or smelled the rotting stench it left behind. Fur as white as snow, legs entirely skeletal as magic ate the skin and tissue away, and its eyes were wide, mirroring the world around it with no life left inside. Maybe once it had been a real doe—maybe some of it still was given how well-formed it looked—but magic had twisted any gentleness away. It was simply a beast now feasting on what magic left the tower of its own accord.

Normally, Carrow dealt with beasts such as this and felt them as soon as they formed, but this one got by unnoticed. And if left alone, it could easily be used to find their tower.

But what worried Nezael in this single moment was that it would hurt Yorick.

It galloped away and Nezael moved after it, drawing his magic tight through his body so he'd be ready to strike. As he rushed through the gap in the trees, after the ghostly frost it left in the air, he met a solid body on the other side. He jolted out of panic, magic slipping out of his fingers in some desperate plea to protect him, but he quickly dispelled it to prevent himself from hurting anyone.

Strong hands had steadied him, almost pushing him up against the tree as though to protect him, and Nezael blinked away the frost clouding the air to see Yorick. He was out of breath, like he'd truly chased after Nezael, and he opened his mouth to speak.

Nezael sighted the beast's ghostly gleam behind Yorick and pushed magic back into his hands. Yorick saw the glow, shocked, and Nezael used the magic to throw them both into the shrubbery. The shock of hitting the ground jolted through Nezael's arm, the impact shivering pain through his wrists and up his shoulders, and Yorick made a pained grunt, but it was better than what the doe had planned. Its ghostly breath blew over them, icicles as sharp as knives forming across the plants in its wake. Nezael pulled himself out from under Yorick's protective arm and forced himself to his feet.

"What is that?" Yorick asked, coming up behind him.

"An accident. Stay there."

Thankfully, Yorick knew how to take direction.

Nezael gathered magic, letting the frost nip his fingers as it formed, and drew the doe's gaze away from Yorick. All it wanted was more magic and Nezael was a source of it. The doe charged with an unearthly growl full of fury while magic twisted its legs to move faster. Nezael shifted quickly, bracing himself, and the beast flew past, leaving a breath of cold, dead air in its wake. Nezael yanked the doe's magic to his will, holding it tight, and morphed it into a current he could use. When he felt the frenzied heartbeat of the doe against his own, he pulled magic from within himself and sent it forward. It manifested as lightning crackling across the lingering frost and struck the doe so brightly, everything flashed white.

But that was it. The magic keeping the doe alive released itself and the doe's body slumped to the ground. It was dead. Color returned to the fur, eating away the snow-white, and a mangled doe lay there as what it had been before the magic. Nezael drew closer and tried to catch the magic dissipating. It was more than simply errant magic, he was sure of it. Magic didn't eat away the legs until they were nothing left but bones and on closer inspection, the doe's chest had been bored through. Dried blood was bright against the fur, but he couldn't tell how long ago it happened.

Nezael's body wavered, suddenly lightheaded.

He would have fallen if a warm arm hadn't caught him around the shoulders. It didn't help his legs folding under him, however, but the arm gently lowered him down. Nezael's vision swam with the movement until he looked up at Yorick peering down at him. Everything stopped when Nezael's gaze was captured within Yorick's. His eyes were a brilliant blue, almost like the summer sky.

"You good there?" Yorick asked.

Nezael swallowed and glanced away. "Yes. Sorry." He exhaled. "It didn't hurt you?" He glanced over Yorick, but found no bit of skin cracked or bleeding.

"I'm perfectly fine." Yorick gently took Nezael's chin

to turn it and Nezael flinched back. "Ah—sorry. Your cheek stopped bleeding. Does it hurt?"

"No." Nezael pressed his hand to it and winced. Maybe a little.

"What do you think made the doe act like that?" Yorick retrieved his arm and Nezael did his best to stay sitting upright on his own. "What did *you* do to it?"

"Magic," Nezael said and his body chilled suddenly hearing it admitted aloud. "Don't tell anyone I was here or what I did or what it was." He tried to stand, but his legs refused to cooperate. Yorick reached out, but paused when Nezael held up his hands. "Don't. Just... please. Don't tell anyone."

"I won't." Yorick gave him a disarming smile. "I'm sure that thing would have killed me at my cabin if it'd found it, huh?"

Nezael nodded and took the moment to memorize Yorick's face. Just in case. It was rugged with an off-center nose, but it was still somewhat youthful beneath the stubble. His cheeks were red, flushed from the cold.

Yorick tilted his head, his smile turning playful. "What?" he asked.

Having been caught, Nezael quickly looked over Yorick's shoulder like it had been his intent all along. Given the way Yorick was still smiling, however, he didn't buy it. Nezael cleared his throat. "How long have you lived there?"

Yorick sat cross-legged, resting one hand on his knee while the other scratched the underside of his chin in thought. "Three years now, I think?" He shrugged. "Place was vacant and the town said I could have it if I made firewood and hunted for meat in the woods." He glanced at the doe. "Think this is safe to use?"

The magic was all but gone. "Likely," Nezael said.

"What about you?" Yorick settled a soft look on Nezael and Nezael's heart jumped. "Are you really some shy wood nymph slinging magic and saving poor saps like me?"

The absurdity brought a chuckle out of Nezael's throat. "Maybe," he said and delighted in the way it made Yorick laugh. It was such a warm sound so unlike his lord's. Endearing, especially the way the motion made his eyes twinkle.

The trees rustled overhead, breaking the moment, and Nezael peered upward. The sky was streaked in orange. He shot to his feet, nearly falling forward. "Oh. Oh no. I have to go." It was late. Much later than he'd thought. He turned, intending to run, but paused as Yorick's hand found his.

"Wait," Yorick said and Nezael looked at him. "You didn't give me your name."

Nezael smiled. "My name is Nezael. It's nice to meet you."

"Nezael." Yorick tested it and Nezael stopped himself from shivering in delight from how it sounded on his lips. Yorick gave Nezael's hand a firm shake, but when he let go, he was patting down his tunic. Curiosity kept Nezael there and Yorick produced a pair of mittens from an interior pocket. "Your hands are cold. Here." He handed them over. "The little old ladies in town make me so many, but be sure to bring those back for me sometime, hm? They're my favorite."

They were a dark burgundy, smelled of cloves, and most of all, warm from being so close to Yorick. Nezael slid them on, hardly resisting another smile, and nodded. "I'll bring them back soon, Yorick," he said, testing the man's name on his own lips.

Yorick gave him a shy little grin and without another word, Nezael hurried away to beat the darkness home, all too aware of the way Yorick watched him go until they could see each other no longer through the trees.

Nezael returned to the tower with the night sky, out of breath, and found his lord frantically throwing on a fur-lined cloak as he hurried outside. The tower's warmth escaped with the opened door, and the orange light inside was shining on Carrow when he sighted Nezael. For one second, Nezael was sure he saw fear in his lord's eyes, but then it melted into something like relief. Carrow swooped Nezael up and wrapped his own cloak around Nezael's shoulders.

He hadn't even realized how much he'd been shivering until then.

"My blossom..." Carrow gently cupped Nezael's face with one hand while keeping the other arm tight across his back. His thumb went over the cracked skin, seeping into it a warmth Nezael had never felt before, and the pain disappeared. "What kept you so long?" He walked Nezael inside as he spoke. "I was terrified."

The doors shut with magic, sealing them inside the tower for the long night. Nezael caught sight of Bellamy ushering Isabella and Agatha out of view down the hall.

"I was merely distracted," he said, the half-lie thick on his tongue. He couldn't risk telling Carrow about

Yorick; his lord would simply drive the man away. Nezael thrust his mittened hands between them and Carrow took a step back, face hardening. "I-I saw these in the market and went back after I finished with Isabella's herbs. I suppose I lost track of the time. That's all."

Carrow eyed the mittens. Relief was replaced easily with suspicion. With gentle fingers, he pulled a mitten from Nezael's hand and dropped it on the floor. Nezael swallowed his knee-jerk reaction to pick it up, especially when Carrow did the same for the other one.

"Bellamy could have knitted you your own," he said slowly and took Nezael's bare hand in his. He inspected the fingers before he gently kissed Nezael's palm, lips tingling with warmth and magic both.

"My apologies," Nezael said quietly. "I—"

"It's done." Carrow released Nezael's hand. "It's too late for lessons tonight. We will reconvene tomorrow morning."

Nezael nodded. "Yes, my lord."

Carrow watched him, but Nezael kept his gaze downcast. On the mittens laying sadly on the floor. "You were so late, we've already put away dinner. I hope in your excursion, you found time to eat."

The warmth from his voice was gone and so was the worry. There was a gulf between them now, like a cold whirlpool sucking in everything, and Nezael's pulse raced. He meekly nodded. "I have eaten," he lied, knowing he'd get no food tonight even if he'd told the truth. May as well pretend he was fine. His stomach ached with the realization he hadn't eaten since breakfast, but it was his own fault.

Carrow's fingers gently touched Nezael's chin and tilted it so Nezael looked at him again. His lord's face was blank. "We'll talk tomorrow morning."

Without another word, Carrow strode away, his warm cloak returned to his arm. Nezael watched him go, as still as could be despite the newfound chill digging into his bones, until the great hall doors slammed shut. The abject disappointment stung and Nezael pressed a palm to his chest to calm his heart. It wasn't the first time his lord had been disappointed, but he'd done so well lately to only throw it away for a kind smile.

A kind smile who'd said his name so fondly. Nezael looked down at the mittens and while he thought to leave them there like his lord likely wanted him to do, he just couldn't. He bent and quickly retrieved them.

He wanted to see the warm smile again.

But tonight, he immediately retired to his chambers.

He washed up in water he found he couldn't warm with magic, redressed in his sleeping clothes which had their warming charm broken, and had just lit the candles across his room when a knock resounded from his door.

Agatha stuck her head in and with her came a small tray of food and mulled wine. She put a bony finger to where her lips had once been and hurried in to settle the tray on Nezael's desk.

Bread slathered with honey and shredded meat from the hen spiced in winter herbs that would make him plenty warm if his room didn't do it, and even a small tart drizzled with raspberry preserves. Nezael smiled at Agatha and she squeezed his arm.

"Next time, don't dally. You know how our lord gets."

She released his arm and nodded to the tray. "Eat up. I'd hate to see you wither away like us."

Nezael caught her hand and gently kissed the knuckles. "Thank you, Agatha."

She tittered and shook her head. "Your charms will get you into trouble, my little lord." She wiggled her fingers at him as she backed out. "Sweet dreams, now."

The door closed and Nezael sat down to eat. He savored each bite in case his lord continued the punishment tomorrow. Everything was perfectly made and he mentally thanked Agatha again and again after each bite. With food in his stomach and the candles twinkling so softly, his room soon became steeped in sleepy warmth. A satisfied sigh left Nezael's lips and he leaned back to look over his room.

His home. Not a very big space, but it was his. There was the vanity beside the desk his lord had gifted him that made the room feel bigger than it was because of the mirror, the walls of bookshelves shoved full of tomes to help Nezael hone his magic (and a few for fun that Isabella had once sneaked in for him), his desk and all the requisite scrolls and ink pens for writing, and then finally his bed. It was in the far corner, taking up the length of the room, and was full of quilts and blankets aplenty, each one full of colorful patterns. The first charm Nezael had learned on his own was how to make his blankets warm throughout the long winter nights.

With food in his stomach rejuvenating his energy, Nezael cast it with a swirl of his hand.

As the magic worked, weaving itself through every stitch of fabric, he gazed out of the windows behind his desk. It was dark, a few stars twinkling above the faraway trees, and the reflection of the candles simply looked like part of the night sky.

His thoughts should have drifted to possible lessons, ways to make it up to his lord to keep him on the straight and narrow path to absolve him of his follies today, but they didn't. Try as he might, the thoughts strayed and landed firmly on Yorick and his smile. The soft touch of his hands. The way it would have been so easy to sit there with him in the forest and talk. After a while, Nezael didn't even mind and let his thoughts linger for as long as they wanted to. It took him all the way to his bed and lasted long after his candles had gone out. Drifted into his dreams.

Because he desperately wanted to see Yorick again and nothing his lord did could take it away.

THREE
HERBS

THE TOWER WAS THICK WITH TENSION THE following day, and Nezael did his best to tiptoe around it. He played the part of a good apprentice with his lord and helped him hone spells and wards for the winter to come. His focus was shot, however, having to forgo breakfast because Carrow immediately drew him into the great hall for lessons. Carrow was sharp and short today and Nezael had to keep from flinching whenever Carrow snatched his hands to show him again and again how to draw the ward correctly. It didn't help Nezael's thoughts were set firmly on last night—furthering the distraction—and as a result, Carrow's temper led the lessons.

"Wrong."

"Stop. Do it again and do it *right*."

"I shouldn't have to reteach you this, my blossom."

And then long stretches of silence as Nezael struggled to concentrate under the piercing gaze of his lord.
By the end of the day, when Nezael's body was weak,
aching from all the attempts and all his constant failures,
he managed to do a single ward correctly. It felt too late
in the day to do something so simply, but it softened
some of Carrow's hard edge and he let Nezael eat dinner.

Once more, Nezael had to force himself not to rush
through the meal and savored each bite like it would be
his last, especially since his lord silently watched him eat
too.

The skeletons kept to themselves, their own prep-
arations keeping them busy, and they had no soft words
to share. Nezael didn't blame them any. He was the one
who incurred Carrow's wrath and so he would have to
deal with it.

Thankfully, after the first day, Carrow's warmth
began to return in pieces until finally, he was the lord
Nezael knew and adored. Nezael's magic concentration
returned in turn and the woodsman became a happy
memory only to be played with in dreams, buried beneath the desire to be a good apprentice. The tension
washed out of the tower and it became the home Nezael
had come to know so well.

When Nezael wasn't cornered into lessons to better
protect himself and experiments with his skeletal bird—
he could now control the trajectory of its flight—he was
with Bellamy, learning how to knit.

Bellamy had been confused at first when Carrow
made the decision—so had Nezael—but self-sufficiency
was hard to come by and Carrow wanted to make sure

no more money was wasted on frivolous purchases. Yorick's mittens were safely hidden in Nezael's room for the day Nezael would take them back. Sometimes, before he drifted off to sleep, he'd retrieve them just to breathe them in. While the clove scent faded day by day, it helped him dream of Yorick again. Maybe when he returned them, he'd have his own gift to give. He just had to figure out knitting first.

Unfortunately, knitting was... well, it did its job. It worked Nezael's hands and kept his thoughts from straying, lest he miss a stitch. Bellamy performed it effortlessly, comfortable in the library couch beside Nezael, and spoke as much as he could as his hands worked seemingly on their own. The yarn quickly became strips and combined into a scarf coiling down his lap. Nezael couldn't quite work as fast until after a few days of struggling, he thought of it like weaving magic.

The spell was deceptively simple. Once he got a hold of the basics, however slow he was at them, he pushed thought and intent into his knitting needles and guided them on how many stitches across and then how many rows. Then, all he had to do was watch it as his magic did the rest. Eventually, his concentration would fray and he'd have to stop, but it worked seamlessly. Bellamy scoffed when Nezael explained it to him.

"Magic defeats the purpose, little lord," he teased.

Nezael waved him off dismissively. "My method is just as valid."

Especially because his method made Carrow's smile return when Nezael took an evening to explain how he'd used what he knew of necromancy as a base to moving the needles on their own. Bellamy still scoffed at the whole display, insisting knitting wasn't to be automated, but Carrow stayed delightfully interested. He never tried it himself, but over the week, he watched Nezael weave the magic necessary, sometimes offering another way to do it that worked better.

By the end of the week, Nezael finished his scarf of dull reds and browns, and also the second, secret scarf he'd worked on at night until he fell asleep. This one was for Yorick and made from greens and whites cabled together. It stayed safely tucked away with the mittens until Nezael could go out to his cabin again.

The morning after finishing his project, Nezael joined his lord in the library and presented his scarf to Carrow. Gently, his lord drew his fingers across the yarn and his eyes tracked the magic still settled within.

"Perhaps I have been too harsh," he mused. "You *are* learning, albeit differently than I had considered." He gently wrapped the scarf around Nezael's neck and smiled softly. "Come spring, you may truly be ready to raise your own human skeleton."

Nezael's heart soared. "Truly?" He sat at the edge of the couch, hardly containing his excitement as his lord leaned back to consider him. "You really think I'd be ready?"

Carrow shrugged and crossed his legs. "You've done a good job with the animals you raised. The cat remembers what it was like to be of the flesh and fur and the bird listens to your direction without hesitation. This scarf shows your mastery over weaving magic in ways I had not considered. So yes, my dear little blossom." His smile widened with true warmth. "Come spring, we will find you a suitable skeleton and you shall show me you're worthy of being called my necromancer." He stood and gently cupped Nezael's head in his hands. "As it happens, ingredients we need only bloom this time a year. I think I've kept you cooped up too long. You're wilting in here."

He bent and retrieved Nezael's spell book from his other side and flipped to the blank pages, past all the other spells inscribed within. Touching his finger down a blank page, his eyes lit with magic and spells unfurled themselves on the page, detailing all sorts of spells related to raising humans and what was needed. Much more than simple will and intent.

"There we are. All I know myself for your perusal over the winter." Carrow returned the tome. "First, I want you to gather the requisite life blossoms from the forest." He turned the page to a plant sketch. It reminded Nezael of a little lantern. "They only grow in the autumn when plants release their own life to either die or sleep throughout the winter. Our stores have run low and we'll need more for your skeleton and for our process of waking ourselves. Find as many as you can and also search for whatever else Isabella needs."

After a pause, likely waiting for Nezael to commit the plant to memory, Carrow took Nezael's back chin in hand to tilt his head to look at him. "Life blossoms are essential and rare. Take heed and search well, my blossom."

"I will, my lord."

~

THE AIR OUTSIDE WAS BITING AND HOWLED AS IT BLEW

through the trees which had lost much of their leaves since Nezael had been cooped up. He hurried into the forest, mittens smelling of cloves covering his hands while layers of furs and cloaks were wrapped around his slight form. He had no idea where to start looking for the life blossoms and neither had Isabella. The plant was incredibly particular about where and when it grew and while part of Nezael thought he should be worried, he wasn't because there was someone who likely knew the forest as well as he did. Someone who he owed a visit to.

Or maybe that was the lie he told himself as his feet led him across the footpaths he'd traveled endlessly in his dreams just to spy Yorick again. Sunlight streamed down golden today, shimmering the frost left in the shadows between the trees, and it made the grove with the cabin warm and inviting.

Yorick was there again, performing the same swings, and Nezael stood at the edge of the forest, mesmerized watching his human body work and he resisted the temptation to run his fingers across it. When Yorick noticed him this time, Nezael didn't run. He simply smiled and when Yorick gave him the same, Nezael took the invitation to come closer and was glad to find Yorick's smile widening as he did so.

"I've come to return your mittens," Nezael said, but made no motion to take them off.

Yorick eyed him and leaned against the axe. "It's still cold. Hold onto them for a while longer." He stiffened as Nezael produced the green and white scarf from beneath his cloak and wrapped it around Yorick's neck.

"I made this," Nezael said, gently tying it in the front

and tucking it into his tunic. "Hold onto it for me too for as long as you need."

Yorick smoothed his fingers over it, but his eyes never left Nezael's. "I can do that." When Nezael looked away, face too warm, Yorick chuckled. "I didn't even know you knitted."

"I didn't until this week." Nezael studied the axe. It was simply made. Nothing remarkable and nor was the blade spelled in such a way to prevent it from dulling. He became quickly aware Yorick watched him with the same curiosity Nezael gave the axe and he pointed. "Don't you have enough wood already? Every time I've come by, you're chopping more."

"It's not for me," Yorick said, nodding to the cart loaded with twined bundles of firewood near his cabin. "One family wanted a few more bundles." He nudged Nezael with his elbow. "You want to try a swing or two? You seem to like watching me."

Nezael's cheeks warmed. "W-What? I—"

Yorick winked, grinning, and Nezael fully turned away to make his cheeks cool off. "I think it's endearing. Here." Yorick gently took Nezael by the shoulders and turned him to the axe. "Take it with both hands like this."

He stood behind Nezael and pressed close as he wrapped his arms in front to help Nezael take the axe with both hands. Nezael *knew* how to hold an axe—it wasn't hard—but his body gave out a delighted shiver as the arms closed around him. With Yorick's body molded against his so closely, Nezael felt the steady heartbeat deep within his chest.

Then Yorick moved away and Nezael tried his best

not to sulk. Yorick picked up a log and set it on the stump.

"Go on; try it," he said and stepped aside to watch Nezael. "Aim for the center."

Nezael pulled the heavy thing aloft, mimicking the motions he'd watched Yorick make just before, and brought it down. The log didn't split at all; it went sideways instead and fell off the stump altogether. Nezael's entire face blazed with embarrassment.

Yorick was snickering and covered his wide smile with his hand as Nezael shot him a look. "Not as easy as you thought, is it?"

Nezael huffed. "You made it look effortless!"

Yorick righted the log and Nezael gave him the axe. In one strike, the log was bisected and Yorick shrugged. "It is for me," he teased and Nezael pushed his shoulder. "I'm sure that lightning you did would have done it in half the time."

"Or set it on fire." Nezael snorted. "I'm not quite that exact with it yet."

"It'd be a sight to see."

Yorick set the axe back in its home and gathered the fallen firewood. Nezael quickly bent to help and with both of them working, they'd soon twined the bundles together and loaded them into the cart.

"Want something to eat?" Yorick asked. "I've got a stew simmering."

Nezael sniffed the air. Beyond the crisp autumn wind, he *did* smell something delectable wafting from the cabin. He eagerly nodded and followed Yorick around to the door. He'd walked in before his rational side told him perhaps this was too much of a distraction and that whisper was buried as Nezael took in the cabin around him.

Even from the outside, he'd knew it be small—barely enough space for one person—but now being inside, the size only made it cozy. Warm honey hued wooden walls were covered in thick tapestries woven with triangle and diamond shapes, all sorts of different earthy tones against a cream color that brightened the space. Right inside, the floor was made of stone and led into a kitchen nook on one end fashioned around the black oven and stove. There was a pot atop the stove and the aroma of stew floated throughout the cabin as it cooked. Windows surrounded the kitchen and peered out toward the trail coming by the cabin.

Past the kitchen, the cabin was raised up by one step with wooden floors aplenty. Rugs of all sorts of muted colors lay across the wood, some more worn than others, but it reminded Nezael of the tower. The ceiling beams were exposed up top and the roof slanted down farther on one side than the other. A bed covered in pillows and quilts was beneath the slanted side and lay horizontally to the window above it. At the foot of the bed a wooden chest carved with a branch design on all sides.

Across the room was a small sitting area complete with a wooden dining table, a couple of chairs on one side, and a thin couch pushed against the wall on the other. Spread across the table were playing cards, books, and candles not yet lit. In the farthest corner of the house was a stone hearth, a fire gently crackling within behind a metal grate. On the stone mantel around the hearth were little wooden knickknacks of animals, each one lovingly carved. Nearby was a single arm chair facing the hearth and it looked about as comfortable as the couches in the tower's library if Nezael had to guess. He was tempted to curl up in it, but refrained.

More than anything else, beyond the aroma of stew, Nezael smelled cloves and cinnamon, even the dried flowers hung from the rafters above. He loved it all and breathed in deep.

"It's not much," Yorick said as Nezael studied everything to memorize it so it may grace him in his dreams. "But it's home. A lot of it was already here when I showed up—I just made it more mine."

Nezael had drifted closer to the hearth and touched one of the wooden figures. A doe still smelling distinctly of wood like she'd just been made. "Everything's lovely. Did you make these?"

Yorick glanced over from the kitchen. "Usually in the summer," he said. "Kids like them, so they're something easy to make and sell."

"They're well crafted." Nezael left the doe with the fawns nearby and continued peering across the room. The books on the shelves near the back were all read through, spines cracked with age, and Nezael held back from pulling them out to gaze upon the pages himself.

"This will be done soon," Yorick said, giving the stew a stir. "Feel free to sit down and get comfortable."

Nezael had never been anywhere that wasn't his tower beyond quick visits to town. He didn't quite know how to be comfortable anywhere else and he glanced at Yorick. The woodsman had taken off his boots, leaving them on the stone floor near the door. Nezael looked down at his own, embarrassed he hadn't done the same, and hurried to do so. Yorick's coat hung on a hook against the door and Nezael left his cloak and furs beside it. Mittens went around the hook as well and looked quite at home.

The cabin was plenty warm without all the layers and Nezael settled in at the table. Yorick continued fussing in the kitchen, humming to himself and Nezael was glad to listen to it. Nezael would have watched the man move, but he thought better about it and instead, brought the candles closer. Magic ignited the wicks with a pinch of his fingers, blooming little twinkling fires to life.

"Does anyone else ever visit?" Nezael asked.

"Sometimes in the summer," Yorick said without much hesitation. "There's this group of aunties who insist on giving me food." He chuckled. "I make them tea when they come and we play a game of cards. Winter's heavy on their bones, so they don't come out this far now."

"Aunties?" Nezael repeated.

"Ah... mothers who miss their grown children? They just tell me to call them auntie this and auntie that." Yorick retrieved two bowls from the cupboards and placed them on the counter. "They're sweet. Maybe they're hoping one day I'll have kids they can dote on or something."

"Do you want children?"

"Hasn't really crossed my mind." Yorick shrugged and glanced at Nezael, lifting an eyebrow. "How about you? Forest nymph who's not a nymph at all?"

Nezael chuckled. "It never occurred to me either. I don't... I don't interact much outside the markets in town and even then, I don't take care to remember anyone." *Except for you.* But he kept that part to himself. He turned away and watched the candle's flames flicker. "I know I live deep in the forest, but I can assure you: I'm as human as you are."

Yorick laughed. "Just what a nymph would say!"

"Oh! Come on!" Nezael couldn't help the laughter bubbling out of his throat. "I've lived here ever since I can remember. I just know magic. Nothing else magical about me besides."

Yorick hummed like he didn't quite believe Nezael and Nezael sighed loudly, making the woodsman laugh again. "Never met anyone who could do spells like what you did," Yorick added. "Charms and whatnot sure—there's this passing sorceress who sells stuff in the summer—but no one's shot literal lightning from their hand."

Or raised the dead, Nezael added to himself and bit back from admitting it aloud.

"You're just something else, you know?" Yorick whispered softly and Nezael chose to take it as a compliment, smiling again.

It wasn't long before supper finished and Yorick brought it over. Two bowls full of stew seasoned with pepper and garlic, rosemary baked bread still warm from the oven, and two cups of mulled wine. Nezael took in the aroma and stirred his bowl; the broth had a thick consistency among the beef, vegetables, and dumplings. Agatha made something like it often when it grew cold. Always did the trick to warm him up. Maybe this would be the same.

"This all smells lovely," Nezael complimented as Yorick sat beside him. "Do you cook a lot?"

"My ma was pretty good at it," Yorick said and nodded to a well-read book in the kitchen. "When I left home, she made sure I took her recipes with me—she has them all memorized. Otherwise, there's a tavern in town I can get something from if I don't mind how loud it is."

Nezael smiled, even if thinking of parents left him hollow. He brushed it aside and hoped Yorick didn't notice as he happily dug in. The bread soaked in the stew and melted in his mouth as he took a bite and the stew itself went down warm, heating him up from the inside. They didn't talk much as they ate, but Nezael didn't mind. He enjoyed being in someone else's company for once. Existing together and being content. Besides, while Carrow's silence bored into Nezael like he'd done something wrong, Yorick's was easy and soft. He liked it.

The meal finished too soon, drawing Nezael back to reality, but therein he found Yorick smiling softly at him.

"Yes?" Nezael asked.

"You just went quiet," Yorick said. "And looked so content there."

Heat bloomed across Nezael's neck and threatened to creep up his face. "No one's invited me to a meal like this," he said and settled his spoon down. "I'm fed fine, make no mistake, but this is... nice. Different, but nice."

"You're welcome to come by any time you want," Yorick said. "Maybe you could teach me some magic. The candles twinkle nicer when you light them."

There it was, all the warmth rushing to Nezael's face, and he tried to hide it by looking at the candle. Teaching magic wasn't possible if the potential wasn't there and in Yorick, it definitely wasn't, but Nezael kept it to himself. "I'd love to." Nezael smiled shyly at him. "I think you're the first person I've ever met on my own."

His gaze drifted to the window, scared of Yorick's expression after having admitted that aloud, and he jolted. Dusk bloomed across the grove in streaks of pinks and oranges. "Oh. Oh no." He almost clattered over his chair attempting to dash back to the door for his cloak and boots. "It's late. It's really late."

"What's wrong?" Yorick was right there, yanking his own boots on too as though he intended to follow Nezael out the door.

"I need special plants," Nezael explained as he laced up his boots. "They're called life blossoms and they bloom at this time each year. They have immense magical properties and I need them."

"I think I know them," Yorick said and Nezael faced him, astonished. "It's used in tea to help with healing. I saw some earlier this week not far."

Nezael nodded fervently. "Please. Show me."

As the sun grew dim along the tips of the trees, drawing dark shadows across the woods, Yorick hurried Nezael through the trails and pointed out the two plants beginning to hum with blooming life blossoms along the river's edge. They shone faintly like firelight, twinkling with magic, and Nezael deftly clipped them with his dagger. Two of them would have to do for now, even if he feared his lord's reaction.

Before Nezael could run back to the tower, panic pushing magic into his legs to make him faster, Yorick took his hand. "Tomorrow," he said, "I can show you more. They're deeper in the woods."

Nezael nodded. "I'll try to come by," he said. "Thank you." He brought Yorick's hand to his lips and kissed the knuckles before he turned and ran through the forest.

It was only when he caught sight of the tower did he realize perhaps it'd been too intimate a motion, but he couldn't take it back now, nor could he return to spy on Yorick's reaction. He had to stay focused.

The sun's light had lowered past the top of the tower and Nezael hurried inside, sad jar of only two life blossoms tight in his arms.

His lord was there inside the door as though waiting for him, although this time he wasn't frantically pulling on a cloak to mount a search. He regarded Nezael coldly as Nezael came inside and when his gaze landed on the jar, his expression hardened.

"I found two," Nezael said, breathless from the run. "I-It was growing dark when I determined another place to search and I didn't want to be late coming home." He held the jar close and couldn't meet Carrow's gaze. "I will find the rest of what we need tomorrow. I promise."

The sigh from Carrow's lips dug deep. "Life blossoms are decidedly rare," he murmured as he drew closer. He tipped Nezael's chin upward to look at him. Carrow was resigned, not annoyed. Small miracles. "You did fine, my blossom. Agatha should be done with supper about now. Go eat."

Nezael blinked. "What about you?"

"I've other matters to attend to." He gently brought a hand through Nezael's hair. "I will speak to you tomorrow once we have acquired the life blossoms." He traced the same hand down to Nezael's cheek. "Am I clear?"

"Yes, my lord."

Have the blossoms tomorrow. That was the command. Nezael didn't want to find out what happened if he didn't or if he let a distraction stray him from this path he'd been on for years. He couldn't throw it away. Not now.

Morning came after a silent evening alone and a fitful night of sleep. Nezael was out of the tower doors without prompting before frost had melted from the grass. Sallow sunrays hardly penetrated the forest today, but even in the dark gray shades of morning, he knew his way to Yorick's cabin by heart.

Yorick wasn't outside this time—the axe was where they'd left it yesterday—and at first, Nezael worried he was gone in the morning, but one knock upon the door proved his worries unfounded. Yorick immediately answered, already dressed warmly, and had the scarf Nezael had knitted around his neck. Nezael smiled, but immediately dashed it aside to hold up his jar.

"You told me you'd show me where the other blossoms were," he said.

"I know," Yorick said, smiling faintly. "I'm sure we'll get enough and more."

Yorick strode through the woods with such ease, Nezael wondered if his lord's wards had ever worked on the man. The magic was certainly there, but the farther ones must have waned over time. If Nezael was sent out to redo them come spring, he needed to make sure to keep it this way. Let Yorick through unheeded. There were ways to and he'd figure it out in time.

The path took him deeper in the woods than he'd ever gone on his own where light receded beyond the branches too thick overhead. With ease, Nezael made a sphere of light in his hands to guide them, and it wasn't long afterward before they found a grove full of life blossoms. Each one flickered like candlelight in the dark. Soft shimmers of magic folded over the petals as they took what was left for them. Soon, Nezael's jar was full enough to be a light of its own and Yorick didn't stop from showing him the other herbs in the grove. All kinds Nezael knew Isabella needed more of and together, he and Yorick clipped all they could into the jar. He did it all the way back to the trail and Nezael was glad for his help, but tried and *tried* to keep from distractions this time. He'd already tested his lord enough.

When they returned to the well-traveled road, Nezael figured it was enough and stopped Yorick from taking him to yet another hidden grove.

"I think this will be plenty," he said, happy with how the jar warmed his fingers. "Thank you. I don't know what I would have done without your help."

Yorick nodded. "My wanderings come in handy," he said and paused. "Are you all right?" Nezael lifted his eyebrows. "You've been distant. Not like you were yesterday."

Nezael shook his head. "I'm fine. I just really, really needed these. I shouldn't have spent so much time at your cabin yesterday." He stopped, taking in a sharp breath seeing the hurt in Yorick's expression. "N-No. I mean—I mean..." He dropped his head, thoughts scrambling in a panic. "I love spending time with you. I swear."

Yorick waited, watching Nezael, but Nezael couldn't look up at him. After too long, Yorick tilted his head. "What are the herbs for?" he whispered, like he feared speaking too loudly.

Nezael hesitated, pressing the jar closer. No lie came to mind.

"Is it for the necromancer?"

Hearing the term out in the open like this made Nezael's heart race and he stared at Yorick, wide-eyed. He'd leaned against the wooden fencing around the road. Holly bushels had been wrapped around the posts like the bridge.

"It's the going rumor," Yorick supplied and gazed at the life blossoms. "That's what it takes to raise a skeleton, right?"

"How do you know that?"

Yorick shrugged. "In the old days, people buried their loved ones with a life blossom so when they met the reaper, they had something to trade. I figure it must have been born from something."

"Life blossoms raise human skeletons by becoming the heart the soul latches onto," Nezael whispered. "Animals are easier—they don't require the same."

Yorick's gaze flitted up to Nezael's and he held it. "Are you a necromancer?"

"Yes," Nezael breathed. "I-In training." He dropped his eyes to the jar, drawing his shoulders tight. "I've never raised a person." He swallowed. "I know people think we're scary, but I swear I would never hurt someone or make them a skeleton against their will."

"You aren't scary," Yorick said.

Nezael let some of the sudden panic breathe out. "Truly?" He peered up at the man and found him smiling gently. "It-It doesn't bother you?"

Yorick shook his head. "No reason why it should. It's a vast world out there with so many different forms of magic." He stepped away from the fence and closed the gap between them slowly as though to show how unafraid of Nezael he was. "I won't say a thing. Promise. No business of mine what you do up there."

"Thank you," Nezael said, relieved. "Thank you." He turned and gazed down the path. "I should return before my lord gets weary of my tardiness."

"Come by again sometime," Yorick said softly. "I like talking to you."

The words struck Nezael in the chest so absolutely, his legs froze. Yorick sounded like he feared Nezael would never come back and on one hand, Nezael understood. They had no reason to come together. Except they were both desperately lonely and craved friendship. Only Nezael hadn't realized how lonely he was until now. The only world he knew revolved around Carrow. It was of secrets, lies, and deception to the world at large. He knew not entirely what Carrow had planned, only that his lord could trust no one but his inner circle and somehow, Nezael was part of it.

It made him lonely in ways he never thought possible until he'd found kindness and smiles in Yorick.

Nezael glanced back at Yorick, more specifically, his lips. There was another moment, a timeless one that felt too long in retrospect, before Nezael stood on his toes and gently pressed his lips to Yorick's and kissed him. Yorick's lips were warm, like all of him probably was, and Nezael withdrew before the kiss led to anything else.

"I like talking to you too," Nezael whispered as Yorick's shock melted into such a soft look like he'd found exactly the answer he'd been searching for too. "I would like many more kisses if you have them for me."

Yorick chuckled. "I think I can find plenty more." He drew Nezael in again, bending lower to kiss him back. It was just as chaste as the first, but pleasure wound through Nezael's entire body this time. To have desire reciprocated like this was something he'd never receive from his lord, he was sure.

"I'll be back then," Nezael said against Yorick's lips. "For all of them."

So he could give just as many back. Nezael hurried away before desire took hold completely and kept him out until dark. Not today. He could wait and let the desire simmer into a small flame. Even if it meant ignoring Yorick's lips. His hands. The muscles in his back so clear in his mind. Yet still, he wished so much he'd given in to the soft, pleading look Yorick gave him as he walked away and returned to follow the woodsman back to his cabin, but it was better this way.

He was a necromancer and his lord awaited.

FOUR

SLUMBER

THERE WAS SOMETHING MORE THAN BEING SIMPLY content now in the tower. Nezael found joy searching through Isabella's stores only so he had a reason to leave. A reason to delve into the woods with Yorick. To steal kisses off his warm lips and watch the way he smiled, any shred of loneliness melting from his shoulders. And, like the good apprentice he was, Nezael returned before night arrived, a hum to his lips and herbs in his bag. He took to Carrow's lessons with carefree ease and wards and glyphs came easier to him. Even Carrow noticed, but was more amused than anything else, and Nezael was glad his lord took the new confidence as it was and thought nothing suspicious. It was infectious too, putting even Carrow in better moods.

The joy seeped into Nezael's dreams and there, he spent them with Yorick. Many times, leaving the forest together with him and never coming back. Those were too much to consider and when those dreams arrived, Nezael quickly buried them to focus on reality. He had a role. He was the dutiful apprentice to the Great Sorcerer Carrow of the Thorns and he'd continue to be. Even if the fantasy of leaving made him warm as the tower drew colder.

"My blossom, you are positively radiant lately," Carrow's voice brought him down from all the potential fantasies and back to one of their final training sessions before winter arrived. Nezael had been learning to ferry messages back and forth using the bird's hollow body. His lord was clear on the other side of the room, delighted after listening to one of Nezael's admittedly more verbose messages.

Nezael laughed, his cheeks warming. "I'm simply excited," he called out as Carrow gently scratched the bird under the chin. The sensation crawled across Nezael's own neck, giving him goosebumps, and he hastened to release his magic hold on the bird. Carrow gave him a knowing look. "My apologies. It's just you'll be teaching me to raise a human skeleton in the spring. I can hardly wait."

Carrow came over, a wistful look in his eyes, and let the bird fly back to its home in the rafters as he went. Nezael had put some fabric up there for the bird and it had already made a little nest for itself. Some imaginary need born of Nezael's desire for it to be comfortable.

"Ah, if only we had the time now." Carrow held Nezael's chin in his hands and tilted it upward. "I thought to suggest you slumber with me so spring comes faster for you, but alas, I need you out here, especially now."

Nezael refrained from answering; before, he'd wanted to sleep like all the rest to make winter disappear faster like his lord said, but now, he couldn't find comfort in the same thought. It meant he'd have to leave Yorick all alone and that thought made him despondent.

"Come spring, my blossom." His lord bent down and kissed him on the forehead. "Now, put your newfound energy to use and help Isabella with her stores."

Nezael eagerly did so, trying so hard not to seem so excited about leaving, but even Isabella took note of his lifted mood and teased him about it.

Unfortunately, he couldn't stay out long with Yorick this time—it was much too late—but they used their time wisely. The herbs were found swiftly and for as long as they could stand it, they stayed together in the trees. Nezael managed at least one breathless kiss from Yorick after so many smaller, teasing ones. And then despite the desire to linger longer, make the memory more than herbs and kisses, the dark was calling him home. What little he managed to touch of Yorick, however, was enough to make him feel as though he floated and for that, it was worth it.

With the kisses still fluttering up and down his neck, burned into his lips, Nezael happily deposited the herbs he'd gathered into Isabella's honeycomb shelves. Still floating almost, he made it into his room before he noticed Isabella had followed him the entire way up.

He jolted in shock when she shut the door after her.

"My little lord," she said teasingly, "what have you been up to out there?"

Nezael stammered, all sorts of lies and excuses disappearing in an instant. "Collecting herbs for you, of course!" It wasn't a lie. Not really.

Isabella watched him and it somehow felt like she stared into his very soul, even without eyes. She drew closer with a confident step and flicked a spot at the crook of Nezael's neck. "Yes, my little lord, but what is this here, then?"

Warmth rushed through Nezael's entire body as he spun to face himself in the vanity. There on his neck was a mark. The spot that had made Nezael squirm with delight when Yorick had pressed his mouth to it. Somehow, Nezael felt warmer, like his very blood was on fire, and all he could do was cover his face with one hand. Isabella was cackling behind him.

"Did you not think it'd happen?" she teased and turned his chin to face her. Out came a container from her breast pocket. "Blood vessels are fragile things. This will help it heal in time." She gathered up the cream on a skeletal finger and liberally applied it. "Be glad our lord has taken absolutely no notice of it."

Nezael frowned. "I'm sure—"

"No, you aren't." Isabella said it so sharply, Nezael snapped his mouth shut. "Believe me, little lord. It's best he knows not of this." She let him go and stepped back to consider him. "You don't have to tell *me* the sordid details, but I do hope you've been smart and having fun most of all. It's what has you in this mood, isn't it?"

Nezael nodded. "Yes, it is," he admitted and there was the sensation like she smiled at him. "Isabella..." He hesitated and tried to piece words together. "Have you ever... um."

She cackled again. "Not in *years*, but when I was alive and among the flesh, I can tell you I've had my share." She tapped a finger on her teeth in thought. "I've no real advice, my little lord, except your heart is a fragile thing and so too is your body. Be kind to both. There's more to this world than our dusty bones cooped up here." She reached out and straightened the neckline of Nezael's tunic. "I think our lords forgets this, surrounded by all our bones day in and day out."

"Except me."

Isabella paused and took her hands away. "Yes, except for you of the flesh variety. I am sure he never forgets this fact." She pressed the container of cream into his hands. "I'll leave this with you, but do tell your friend to take it easier on your skin or at least direct him somewhere less noticeable." She pressed her cheek up to Nezael's before drawing back. "Sweet dreams, my little lord. I am glad to see the smile gracing your face so brightly these days."

Nezael couldn't help but smile again as she left.

~

NEXT WEEK, THE DAYS BEGAN WITH A DUSTING OF SNOW clumping in the grass and among the branches, and before Nezael knew it, the solstice had come, heralding in the longest night of the year. It was then all the skeletons except Bellamy slumbered safely inside the tower walls. While Bellamy oversaw his brethren, wrapping them carefully in silks and quilts and applying the sleeping drought inside their skulls, Nezael tended to his lord.

It wasn't often Nezael entered Carrow's chambers and every time, Nezael tried to commit it to memory. Larger than Nezael's own room, but somehow more crammed with books overflowing the bookshelves, a large table of maps of different countries and kingdoms off to one side, a larger canopied bed in the center, and notes for spells all over the place. The single large circular window in the room overlooked the front of the tower, the glass frosted over at the edge now from the chill. Candles were lit, twinkling bright in the coming dark, and afforded Nezael just enough light to help dress his lord in fine robes layered over one another. It reminded him of the old burial rites he'd read about, how often people of power were dressed in one expensive robe after another to keep them warm when the reaper came for them. Carrow was not dead, however; he simply needed to stay warm while he slept.

"Come summer, my blossom," Carrow spoke as Nezael worked a sash around his torso to tie, "this will all change for us." Carrow watched him diligently, arms loose. "No longer will we merely survive in this drafty tower or have to hide in plain sight." When Nezael finished, Carrow cupped his face and tilted it upward. "We'll take our world back once more. This I promise."

For so many years, Nezael never questioned Carrow or his plans. Now, one of *why* nearly tumbled out of his lips—why wasn't it simply enough they were alive? Happy?—but he bit it back. His lord knew what was best for them and he'd trained himself to trust the man. He nodded, turning his head slightly, and kissed the inside of Carrow's palm. It made his lord smile softly and let go.

"I can't wait," Nezael said. "Maybe we could travel with everyone then."

"Perhaps. It has been such a long time."

Carrow turned for his desk stuffed in the corner beside them. Like everything else, it was covered in sketches of wards and sigils, both old and new, but what he searched for was in one of the locked drawers. Upon his touch, the lock twisted with magic and he retrieved a silver necklace from within. A tiny charm of a looking glass hung from it, glimmering in the candlelight. Carrow beckoned Nezael closer.

Nezael bowed his head and Carrow slid the dainty chain twice around his neck so the charm rested in the hollow of his throat. It was cold, but only for a moment before Carrow touched it. Magic softened the chill and Carrow turned Nezael toward the wardrobe where a long mirror hung. The charm looked nice there against his skin.

"Wear this while I sleep," Carrow whispered into Nezael's ear. "It will protect us." He kissed Nezael cheek and the door opened.

Bellamy came in and was as immaculately dressed as ever. Real delight bloomed across Carrow's face and Nezael watched as Bellamy dutifully helped Carrow into bed. The need to recharge his magic made his body weak and Nezael hadn't realized it was so bad. Nezael helped cover his lord in quilts until the man was simply buried in them.

"I am quite warm, you two," Carrow insisted.

"And yet you'll still complain you're cold when you awake," Bellamy teased in return. He tilted himself

toward Nezael and lowered his voice. "He *always* does."
As Carrow chuckled, Bellamy handed Nezael the small
bottle of sleeping draught.

What Isabella had been working on all week. It put
people in such a deep sleep, nothing could wake them
but a burst of magic and life blossom petals. It was why
Nezael had to stay awake; if he didn't, both he and
Carrow would sleep until the end of time, forever preserved in dreams. A little scary, now that Nezael thought
about it. He unstopped the bottle. It smelled of chamo-
mile and lavender and the surface shimmered.

"Here, my lord." Nezael gently placed one hand at
the back of Carrow's head and offered him the potion.
"Sleep well and I will be here to wake you come winter's
thaw."

"Goodnight, my blossom," Carrow whispered and
then drank. It wasn't long before his gaze softened and
his eyelids shuttered closed. His breathing evened into a
deep, slow rhythm, and he was asleep.

Nezael still watched the slight rise and fall of his
chest, worried. What if it'd been too much? Before he
could voice the sudden worry—he'd never gone an entire
winter without his lord's guidance—Bellamy pressed a
hand to Nezael's shoulder.

"It's done," Bellamy said and drew Nezael a step
away.

Magic blew out the candles around them like a sigh
fluttered through the room. The power continued
around them like it was alive, and webs threaded across
everything. They were bright, glimmering all sorts of
colors like a prism, and weaved together glyphs and

wards all across the room and more importantly, Carrow. Bellamy took Nezael back step by step, as though not to disturb the process, and soon they were out in the hall. Magic continued along without them, building fortifications, and Bellamy sealed it all in by shutting the door.

Immediately, a ward formed upon it, bright and golden. Nezael was tempted to touch it and learn how exactly it'd been made, but Bellamy caught his hand.

"Leave it," Bellamy said. "Our lord's magic is gathering what is inert around us to refill him and also protect him." He faced Nezael, tilting his head. "Ever since he found you, he hasn't slept like this. It'll do him some good." It felt like Bellamy smiled, the sound of his voice shifting into something light. "You are young yet. You won't need something this drastic for a long time."

Nezael raised his eyebrows. "All because I'm young? That's it?"

"And well gifted in ways our lord is not despite his desire otherwise," Bellamy said. "You're coming into a mastery of your magic he'd only achieved well into his years. Our lord was truly blessed the day you arrived."

Nezael watched Bellamy, hoping for more—he hardly knew the circumstances of how he came here or much about his lord's past—but Bellamy turned and headed down the hall. Nezael hesitated and glanced at Carrow's door. The ward had grown into an intricate network of runes etching the doorway in gold.

He supposed the past was past. Nezael hurried after Bellamy and followed him down the stairwell.

"What now, then?" he asked as he caught up. "Normally, our lord has things for me to do."

Bellamy shook his head. "And I do not. I am going to do my usual: knit and read. You go eat what Agatha made and then join me in the library when you've finished." He glanced back at Nezael and once more, it felt like he smiled. "There are tomes our lord left out for you to read. Perhaps you could start by learning a thing or two."

Nezael couldn't help but snort. All he ever did was study.

"Or," Bellamy said with a laugh in his throat, "do what your heart desires. This time is yours, my little lord, and not mine to dictate."

Bellamy left him there, mulling over the words, and Nezael peered out the window across from the stairs. Darkness had covered the gardens and it was much too late to go out now, but maybe he could tomorrow when the sun emerged. Do what his heart desired. The thought put a smile on his lips and he decided yes, that was what he'd do, and headed to the kitchens to dine on the supper Agatha had left him before she slept.

FIVE
Snow

S NOW STILL HAD YET TO FALL IN EARNEST AND AFTER A
rather enlightening breakfast (Nezael burned the
bread trying to toast it and the oatmeal turned out
runny), Nezael had no idea what to do with himself.
Bellamy easily found comfort in the same monotony,
especially since he was using his library access privilege
to knit in the comfiest seats in the tower (according to
him). After testing the wards, he was already three books
in and was knitting a blanket. For lack of anything else to
do, Nezael tested the wards too—even the ones outside—
finding them strong still.

Nothing to do left him listless. The idle thoughts led
to thinking of Yorick and those thoughts egged him to
act, even though he'd never left the tower during the
winter.

Do what your heart desires.

Nezael certainly knew what his *body* desired. Maybe that was enough and it drew him down to Isabella's chambers, looking for a reason to leave.

Her stores were full—courtesy of himself and Yorick. He chewed on his lip, looking them over one more time, and they remained full no matter how long he stared. He glanced at Isabella's sleeping form in her bed, wrapped in glinting magic, and then back to her stores. He mouthed an apology for disturbing it and took a jar. She had gathering bags all over the back wall of her room and he dumped half the jar's contents into one, resolving to come back for it later. No one would ever know.

Well, except the cat. It rubbed up against Nezael's leg and he bent down to pet its forehead. Magic reacted in kind and the cat headed back to sleep next to Isabella. It'd watch over her; it always did.

"Our secret," Nezael whispered.

He raced to the library. "Bellamy!" he called out as he entered. Bellamy peered up from his project, the yellow and orange yarn gliding from needle to needle as he worked. Nezael held up the mostly empty jar. "We didn't finish gathering."

Bellamy tilted his head. "Truly?" he asked. "Izzy's usually so good at that."

"I should gather the rest before the snow comes." Nezael pressed the jar close as Bellamy watched him with suspicion.

"It's due to snow any time now," Bellamy argued slowly. "Our lord—"

"He'll never have to know," Nezael insisted, pulse

pounding in his ears with each lie. "First sign of snowflakes and I'll run home." There was a chirp from the top of the bookshelves and he gazed upward. His little bird was there and he smiled at it, happy for its intrusion. He held out a finger for it and it came, settling eagerly upon it. "I even have my bird so I can send you a message if I cannot return in time."

The yarn almost tugged from Bellamy's hands and he looked downward. The cat had followed Nezael up and was now making itself a nuisance. Nezael bit back from laughing.

"You stop that now," Bellamy said and sighed when the cat simply batted at the yarn faster. He gave up, leaving the yarn, and stood to approach Nezael.

"You can go under one condition," Bellamy said and Nezael nodded quickly. "If the snow is falling too fast, you know where town is. Seek shelter there." He fished a hand into his pocket and produced a small coin pouch.

Nezael took the offered pouch and raised his eyebrows. "Truly?"

"Last resort," Bellamy said. "I'd rather an alive little lord than a dead one." He turned and picked up the cat. Some of the yarn had entangled itself in its ribs. "If I lost you, I cannot imagine how cross our lord would be."

It was said so sarcastically, Nezael couldn't quite take it seriously. He smiled all the same. "Thank you." He surprised Bellamy with a hug and received the briefest squeeze back before both hands went back to helping the cat. "I'll be back soon."

"See to it you are."

~

THE GRAY SKIES ABOVE COULDN'T DULL NEZAEL'S MOOD today. Bundled up from the cutting winds, he practically floated through the forest all the way to Yorick's cabin. Unlike the many times before, Yorick wasn't idly waiting for him on the stump and Nezael disliked how lonely the grove looked without his warm smile. It made sense, though; even he knew Nezael had already refilled all of Isabella's stores. There was no reason for Nezael to be here, all things considered. Nezael lingered a moment at the stump, doubts begging him to reconsider, before he decided to head up to the cabin door.

He hadn't been inside since spending dinner with Yorick and Yorick hadn't invited him in again. Maybe he'd been worried for Nezael's own sake, or perhaps something else.

Lingering aromas of cinnamon and sugar drifted around the cabin and Nezael breathed in deep. Yorick must have been baking something with what he'd purchased from town the last time he and Nezael went. All the shopkeepers had adored him and had weighed his arms down with so much to keep him healthy in the cold. Nezael only wished they'd treated him with the same kindness.

Nezael's stomach grumbled and he took that as a sign to knock and see if Yorick would be willing to share.

The door opened shortly, letting warm air wash out with more cinnamon floating along it, and at first Yorick looked confused seeing Nezael. Warranted perhaps, but the confusion melted when Nezael gave him a shy wave.

"Hey you," Yorick said and smiled against the kiss

Nezael immediately gave to the side of his mouth as they went in together. "More herbs already?"

"Not this time." Nezael moved aside as Yorick shut the door. The warmth inside was almost overwhelming, but was much better than the biting cold outside. "I wanted to see you. I was bored by myself."

Yorick snickered as he headed back to the kitchen. Nezael shed a few of his layers, hanging them neatly on the hook beside Yorick's own things, and left his boots next to Yorick's before he followed. Yorick was pulling out a tray of spiral rolls baked with cinnamon and sugar from his oven. Their aroma filled the cabin tenfold and Nezael's mouth watered. Yorick must have noticed; he nudged Nezael teasingly.

"Help me put icing on them?"

There was something about Yorick's tone of voice today, the stilted way he moved, and Nezael watched him a moment. He was clearly nervous despite the smiles and Nezael had no idea why. "I'd love to as long as I get to have one myself."

"I suppose I can't very well eat them all on my own."

Some of the unease melted, at least, and Yorick happily showed Nezael how to drizzle the sugar icing across the top. There were four rolls altogether, practically as large as Nezael's face, and while they were a little misshaped with none of the perfect swirls of the bakery in town, Nezael found them endearing.

Icing didn't take long, but then Nezael had to wait for them to cool further before he could *eat*. Yorick wasn't even swayed by the sad look Nezael gave him and shuffled him to the dining table to sit.

Yorick's lips made the time go by faster. They tasted like sugar and Nezael happily drank it in, pressed against the cushions. Finally, as Nezael's body filled with enough pleasure to overflow, Yorick pulled away and brought the rolls over. It must have been on purpose, the way Yorick was grinning as he did so, but Nezael refused to complain and instead happily accepted the cinnamon roll peace offering. They sat together on the couch, as close as possible while still letting them eat, and Nezael liked it.

The place felt like home, somehow. Some of the dust and cobwebs had been dealt with since he was in here the first time, making it more inviting, and though Nezael missed the few messes he'd seen before, he kept the thought to himself.

They ate quietly, the roll gooey and overrun with icing, and Nezael took his apart with his fingers. Yorick did the same, but his gaze was distant and it felt like there was something he wanted to say. Nezael slowly finished his piece, licking the icing off his fingers, and eyed Yorick all the while. Definitely distracted. He'd picked his roll to pieces instead of eating it, leaving a small mess on his plate.

Gently, Nezael leaned into him.

"Did I do something wrong?" he asked.

Yorick blinked and his shoulders tensed. "N-No—of course not."

"Then what's wrong?"

Yorick stammered, his jaw tensing with words unsaid, and he eventually sighed and thumped back against the cushions. Nezael followed him back and gently took one of his hands to hold while Yorick gathered his words.

"What... what are we?" Yorick asked, staring straight ahead. "D-Don't get me wrong. I've enjoyed your company immensely... I... I didn't actually think you'd be back Then here you are and I'm just confused, I guess."

"You didn't think I'd be back?"

Yorick looked at him with such sadness in his blue eyes. "Every time you visited me, you had something you wanted. I didn't mind. I liked kissing you and I liked helping." He turned back to his roll and excavated a piece slathered in icing with his fingers. "I figured when you finished, that'd be it. I believed thinking otherwise would be lying to myself."

"I needed excuses to leave," Nezael insisted, wishing Yorick would look at him again, but he just ate the piece of roll he'd broken off. An excuse to do anything but see the hurt in Nezael's eyes. "If I didn't have one, my lord wouldn't have let me." He gently turned Yorick's face so he could catch his gaze again. "All I wanted—all I really wanted all this time—was to be yours."

Some of the unease began melting from Yorick, but he didn't answer.

Nezael took Yorick's other hand, the one with icing coating the fingers, and considered it. "Are you so used to being lonely that me never coming back was your only answer?"

Maybe it was too personal a question, especially because Nezael already knew the answer deep down. It was easier to pretend that was all there was to it. To save Yorick from hurting himself by getting attached to a flighty nymph-like necromancer flitting in and out of his life like the breeze. Nezael *did* feel guilty all he'd done was come by when he had an excuse; he should have eschewed them altogether and visited simply to sit inside with Yorick on cold mornings. Watch the frost melt and the sun move across the sky. Show him someone cared about him while needing nothing else in return.

Yorick peered at their hands. Nezael didn't need an answer; he already had it.

Nezael brought Yorick's hand closer and Yorick stiffened, eyes darting right back to Nezael's with a question. Carefully, before he lost his nerve, Nezael slowly slid the finger into his mouth. Yorick went somehow stiller, like he hardly even breathed, and Nezael watched his eyes as he slowly drew the finger back out, running his tongue softly along it to catch the icing.

"I want you," Nezael whispered.

"Oh," Yorick breathed out the word, but remained impossibly still as though his entire body had forgotten how to function.

Slower than the first, Nezael slid the second finger into his mouth, never once breaking eye contact with Yorick even as it went deeper. There was the jolt of a pulse there, Yorick's breathing coming out a little more rapid, and Nezael ever so slowly pulled the finger from his mouth, taking care to catch more of the icing.

"Every single part of you: I want," Nezael said.

"*Oh.*" The word came out more well-formed, Yorick watching Nezael's mouth like it was the only part of him that existed. His eyebrows shot up, realization dawning on him, and his breaths came even quicker. His heartbeat fast in his chest.

"I am surprised the kisses did not give it away," Nezael teased and went for the next finger, the last one with icing still left on it. Not as much, but that wasn't quite why Nezael was doing it.

"I thought you were being polite," Yorick said, barely able to stop the chuckle in his throat, and Nezael made a show of rolling his eyes as he began to pull the finger back out. "You know, I've a mind to tell you where else you can put your lips exactly like that."

Nezael's cheeks burned at the insinuation, even if that had been exactly his intent, and he grinned mischievously at Yorick. "Do you, now? Pray, tell me about it in detail."

Blush bloomed quickly across Yorick's cheeks and he laughed loudly. It sounded like he was darting through the forest with Nezael again—wild and free—and Nezael took it as an invitation to be bolder. He swung one leg around Yorick's lap and firmly placed himself atop it, delighted as he felt a reaction from what awaited him below.

"Would you have me, then?" Nezael cupped Yorick's face to look up at him. "All that I am and more?"

A devilish smile spread across Yorick's lips, like he was really considering everything he wanted to do, and a delighted shiver ran down Nezael's spine. Yorick's hands firmly found their way to Nezael's behind and squeezed it, sending another flush of pleasure straight through Nezael and his pulse quickened.

"I'll have you. All of you," Yorick whispered.

Nezael meant to bend low and kiss him, but then his gaze caught the flurry of white outside. He gasped against

Yorick's lips instead, and threw himself off the couch as fast as he could. He would have fallen outright if Yorick hadn't caught him.

"It's already snowing?" Nezael whispered.

Yorick glanced out the window. It had already coated the grass and more and more fell, looking like curtains from the sky. "It's not safe to go back now," Yorick said quickly. "You can stay."

Nezael's panic calmed, a little realization setting in, and he hid the smile on his lips with his hand. Maybe this was preferable. Yorick saw the smile anyway, understood the intent of it, but before he could draw Nezael in to go back to what was so rudely interrupted, Nezael went to the door.

"One moment—I want to send a message."

The bird couldn't be far when magic kept it afloat. Nezael even felt it, a little twinkle in the snowstorm. He gently opened the door, Yorick watching with more curiosity than anything else, and Nezael drew his hand into the cold. There was a rattle of bones, the slightest hum of a song, and the skeleton bird landed on his finger, no worse for wear. Nezael pulled it close, gently petting its head with his finger to ignite more magic inside its tiny body, and pressed his lips to the cold bones.

"Bellamy, I have adequate shelter. Do not worry for me," he whispered, magic ghosting across his words like a melody. "I will return when the snow ceases. I promise." He hated adding the last part, knowing Yorick was listening, but he feared Bellamy worrying too much without it.

The bird shuffled unseen feathers, Nezael's magic

voice coiling into the empty space in its ribcage, and Nezael kissed its head before he let it fly for its home in the tower. Magic would protect it, this he knew, and very shortly, Nezael lost sight of it in the squall.

Snow spilled inside around him until Yorick saw sense and drew Nezael away to close the door. It was all Nezael could do to toss his worries away and it helped when he turned to take in Yorick in his entirety.

His strong shoulders, his soft chest, and the muscles lining his arms and legs. Yorick was looking at Nezael the same; desire and fire lit up in his eyes. One of them had to start. Nezael pulled him in, kissing him deeply, and before he knew it, his back was on the nearest flat surface—the table, he distantly realized but perhaps it never mattered—and he'd wrapped his legs tightly around Yorick, holding him there as closely as he could until the only option Nezael had was to come up for air. And even then, Nezael wasn't sure if he'd do it if it meant pulling away from Yorick.

~

IT GREW DARK, ONLY THE FIRE IN THE HEARTH PROVIDING light at all, and even it dulled while Nezael acquainted himself with every inch of Yorick's body and the way it reacted to him. What made it shiver, what made the soft moans on Yorick's lip turn to song, and then all the tastes therein. Yorick had done the same with Nezael, learning very quickly what made him tremble, cry out in pleasure, and how eagerly Nezael wanted to take him in entirely. Over and over again until they were both breathless upon the bed, tangled in the sheets. The first touch had sent all sensations spilling forth—desire made apparent

and manifested in their roaming hands and mouths—
and Nezael wished he'd been bolder long before now.
The real Yorick was so much better than all the teasing
dreams. The heat of his body was all encompassing, the
way the weight of it pushed up against Nezael's own body
so true and right each time, and nothing could replicate
it but reality.

He was breathless again when Yorick took himself
away from the bed. The man's skin glistened around the
teeth shaped marks Nezael had left for him. The same
peppered Nezael's own body and this time, he wouldn't
have to hastily hide them for fear of his lord seeing them.
The dim light illuminated the sheen of Yorick's body, the
golden hues all over, and he bent to retrieve the pants
he'd long since discarded. A shame. Nezael rested his
head on the pillow, watching as Yorick pulled them on
before heading over to throw more wood into the fire.

Nezael didn't want to move yet, even as the room
bloomed in new light. His legs were still trembling too
much from all the excitement and moving meant leaving
the bed. Maybe if he looked despondent enough at the
loss of his sleeping partner, Yorick would come back for
yet another round.

Yorick turned and caught Nezael's gaze with a smile.
"Thought you'd fallen asleep." He returned to the bed
and bent to steal a kiss.

"Hungry?" he asked.

Nezael thought about it and rolled over to prop
himself up on his elbows. "Is it cheating if I say for you?"
he asked and Yorick laughed, shaking his head. "I suppose I am as long as it means afterward you come back

to bed. I don't think you're finished with me yet."

It earned Nezael another kiss and Nezael drank it in, this time biting Yorick's lip when he dared to move away.

As Yorick fussed about in the kitchen, likely searching for something easy to make, Nezael noticed the forlorn cinnamon rolls on the counter.

"What about the rolls?" Nezael asked.

"I was hoping to have some tomorrow," Yorick admitted. "Besides, I don't think I could handle watching you eat them again right now." He winked at Nezael, prompting a sudden laugh out of Nezael's throat. When he turned away again, he brought out bowls alongside a sealed jar of what looked like soup.

"This won't take too long." Yorick glanced back. "Think you can handle the wait?"

Nezael rolled his eyes, waving his hand, and the kitchen lit up from the flame on the stove. As Yorick worked, Nezael stretched himself on the bed now cooling without both of them there. Yorick had thrown his clothes this way and that, but Nezael had been buried in complete delight—from Yorick's hot, breathy kisses starting at his neck and working their way lower with each article of clothing discarded—he hadn't paid attention to where they'd fallen. All he had was the necklace his lord had given him. Cool to the touch from protective magic rushing through the links. A little too secure to be ripped off, but Yorick had happily kissed around it like it wasn't there.

However, it wouldn't be proper to eat with only a necklace. Yorick had found his own pants, so there had to be something within arm's reach.

What Nezael found was Yorick's tunic and figured it would do just as well. He pulled it on, carefully moving to the edge of the bed. It dropped past his thighs. Decent enough.

"Hey." Yorick was laughing from the kitchen. "That's my shirt!"

Nezael teased him by pressing it flat against himself. "You took it upon yourself to lose my clothes like a beast," he said and Yorick shook his head, exasperated. "You've no one to blame but yourself. Besides, you'll only tear them off again should I find them." He stood, glad his legs didn't fold from feeling like they were made of jelly, and softly stepped across cabin to the only other thing warm inside—Yorick himself.

"Can I help?" Nezael asked, draping his arms across Yorick.

"I know what your help is," Yorick teased, edging him back before he could get his hands any lower. "You'll just distract me with it." The soup was already simmering over the flame and once he had it covered with a lid, he turned to press a kiss to Nezael's cheek. His gaze went down to Nezael's neck. "Did you always have this necklace? I don't recall your neck being so cold when I kissed it before."

Nezael touched it, feeling the chill anew, and he shrugged. "A recent gift to my lord before he slept," he said. "There's *some* magic on it. I think it's to protect me."

"Not from me, I hope."

"Well, you've touched me just about everywhere and nothing's happened, so I think you're safe." Nezael leaned on the counter, trying to resist dragging Yorick back to bed.

"How long have you been with your lord, anyway?" Yorick asked as he went searching for some bread in the other cupboards. The loaf he pulled out smelled like cinnamon, but not as much as the rolls did.

"I'm not sure," Nezael answered. "I never really kept track of the years until recently. Magic does funny things to aging anyway." He folded his arms and tried to push down the shudder working its way up his legs. The floor was cold. "How'd you end up here?"

Yorick shrugged and placed the bread in the slot below the stove to warm it up. "My da was a butcher and my ma was a baker. I didn't want to do much of either, so since I had a bunch of younger siblings who could carry on the name, I just started to wander." He pulled away the lid from the pot and tasted a spoonful. "I always felt listless no matter where I went until I came here." He smiled, glancing at Nezael. "It's a quiet life, but I'm starting to like it this way."

Nezael returned the smile. "Good. I'd hate for you to wander away now."

Yorick chuckled. "You could come with, you know. Once you learn all you need to from your lord, you could come see more of the world with me."

It wouldn't work like that in the least, but Nezael kept reality to himself. "Maybe," he whispered, but seeing the way Yorick frowned, he must have heard Nezael's unease. Nezael sighed and shook his head. "Let's not ruin the night," he whispered. "I want to live in the present. With you."

"I'd like that," Yorick said softly.

Dinner was a short reprieve before Nezael was rolling across the bed with Yorick pressed so close to him, tasting the life on his lips. The rest of the world didn't matter here, only what they could do for one another in the dark. It simply felt like it was meant to be, the ease at which they acclimated to one another and the way their breaths made music between them.

And on and on into the dark until they needed to breathe, only to find themselves falling for the allure of one another again like the desire was never ending after being pent up for too long.

Morning came bright and glittering over the fallen snow. Nezael didn't *want* to leave, not really, but his body was too pleasurably sore, so another round was not likely. Besides, Bellamy would be worried no matter what message Nezael had sent if he chose to stay out longer. Nezael could always return and he *would*, especially knowing what awaited him here in Yorick's embrace.

Yorick peppered him with soft kisses as he helped Nezael dress, lingering against the more sensitive spots until Nezael had to tell him to stop or else he'd lose half the day reciprocating the touches on Yorick himself.

The last kiss pressed delicately to Nezael's lips as Yorick wrapped the cloak around his shoulders. "Come back soon," he said, hopeful.

Nezael kissed him in return. "I will. Always and forevermore."

It was maybe a few more kisses before Nezael made it out the door and into the bright winter morning. The cold ghosted across his cheeks, but nothing would erase the warmth still coiling through his body. For once, life felt decidedly different. New. Entirely his. And all he'd needed was a friend. Something more. Much more.

Maybe wandering would do him some good.

There was a whole world out there and he'd only seen a glimpse of it shut up inside his tower. And now, he wanted everything else he couldn't see and more. Maybe Yorick could help him do just that.

SIX

WILD

THOUGH EVERY TRAIL AND PATH WAS SNOW-RIDDEN and glittering, covering all Nezael knew of the woods, his lord's wards were beacons and he dutifully followed them home. It stood out, all bark-colored brick and windows gleaming the sun back, and Nezael studied it for a moment before he strode inside. Bellamy was there in seconds, likely hearing the door open, and once he saw Nezael, he placed a bony hand to his chest in relief.

"I told you I'd be back," Nezael said, smiling. "No need for such worry."

Bellamy's shoulders dropped. "I fear I will *always* worry," he said. "Come. The snow weakened some of the wards and you'll need to reapply them before we hunker down by the fireplace with something warm to eat."

Nezael stopped in Isabella's room first and returned

the misplaced herbs, mouthing her a thank you for the opportunity. When he reemerged, he took to Bellamy's directions with ease, his entire being still feeling like it floated from the night before.

Wards came easily to his hands, making the cold recede back beyond the windows, and once they were all fixed, Nezael settled in for the dinner now turned lunch Bellamy had cooked for him the previous night, now all warmed up. It was a small brisket—Nezael didn't exactly know what kind—drizzled in a berry sauce that made the kitchen smell wonderful.

The meal as a whole was a quiet affair and they only spoke about small things. Bellamy regaled Nezael with stories from before Nezael came to the tower, each one more ridiculous than the last to make Nezael laugh, he was sure, and normally, he'd be a rapt audience. Except today his thoughts strayed right back to Yorick and firmly stayed there throughout the rest of the day.

In the night, he dreamed of Yorick in his bed with him and the dreams morphed to match who Yorick was in reality. Nezael could picture him perfectly. The sleepy look in his eyes as it reflected the hearth's light. The soft ghost of his kisses pressing against Nezael top to bottom and it didn't let up until Nezael awoke alone.

The same bright sun and skies as blue as Yorick's eyes heralded the morning, and Nezael had to see him again.

He'd managed to hide another set of herbs, but before he could emerge to show Bellamy they'd missed yet another jar, the skeleton met him halfway up the stairwell.

"Little lord..." Bellamy sighed, shooing him back down into Isabella's chambers.

"I was checking the stores," Nezael said, not quite a lie. He showed Bellamy the empty jar and the skeleton simply shook his head. He went over to exactly where Nezael had hidden the herbs and gave him a look.

"Lies do not suit you."

Nezael's pulse raced, thinking of possible excuses, but none came. Bellamy watched Nezael for so long in silence, it was a relief when he sighed again.

"You can go," Bellamy whispered, taking the jar. "I know the glow of new love, my little lord, though I've not felt it in years." He cupped Nezael's cheek with one hand. "All I ask is you return before dark and keep up with your tower duties. Promise?"

Nezael let go of all half-formed lies and smiled. "Promise."

Though tempting, Nezael didn't go every day. Bellamy seemed lonely when he headed out and even Yorick chided him for leaving the poor skeleton all alone when Nezael confessed his worry. It didn't stop Yorick from eagerly pulling Nezael into bed for a quick romp, however, and Nezael never found it in him to say no— he enjoyed it far too much.

Going between Yorick's cabin and his tower became Nezael's new normal. Sometimes the days were full of desire and want, while the others not so much. Quiet and contemplative, instead. Nezael enjoyed practicing magic while Yorick watched and he even helped Yorick take to the forest to hunt. They never found anything much, but it was freeing to try anyway. In the tower, Nezael stayed with Bellamy and learned magic from his impressive notes after watching Carrow for so long, listened to his long rambling stories, and even knit Bellamy's way to appease the skeleton. Nights were spent studying magic until his thoughts drew too distracted and he fell into the blissful dream awaiting him.

There were, of course, flurries of snowfall which fell so heavily, they barred Nezael from returning to Yorick for a time, but with each one, he sent his bird with a soft message for Yorick's ears only. While Yorick couldn't send messages back, the bird always returned and nipped affectionately at Nezael's finger when he drew it inside.

Weeks into winter, one particular flurry took three days to end. In that time, Nezael honed his spell work, drew lightning in the air as effortlessly as his lord, and practiced his runes. Boring and banal, all things considered, and he was overjoyed to find clear skies and the sun once again shining through his window. Bellamy even let him go out without fuss this time, only making sure Nezael was warm.

The snow had piled itself upon tree branches, weighing them down. Not to mention all the paths covered the same. Nezael had to trudge through the snow to find his usual path. Magic helped once he grew tired, and holding it before himself melted the snow to something more manageable to stomp through, but relying on it too much would wear him out before he found Yorick's cabin. He finally made it by noon, sun bright overhead, and as he raised his hand to knock, the door pulled open. Yorick nearly ran Nezael down, panicked.

"What's wrong?" Nezael asked.

Yorick was dressed to travel the cold. Cloak pulled across his shoulders, the scarf Nezael had made for him tucked around his neck, and his thicker boots and gloves.

"Before the snow flurry came," he started, speaking the words fast as his gaze darted across the forest behind Nezael, "people from town mentioned something was stalking the river's edge. They're scared and no one's been able to figure out what it is or where it came from. It only left a rotting stench and that's it."

Nezael's skin prickled. "Like the doe..."

"Exactly." Yorick took Nezael's hands. "Please, help me find the source. If something like that gets into town, they're defenseless."

The town had never been a priority before; Carrow always regarded it with disdain despite the use it had and Nezael never cared. But people lived there. People like Yorick. Those who didn't deserve whatever this magic beast might do no matter if his lord cared or not.

Nezael nodded and laced his fingers with Yorick's. "Of course. Let's head back to my tower first. I think I have a way to find out where the beast went."

The wards let Yorick through so long as he held Nezael's hand. They shivered and reconfigured, making room for him, and Nezael ignored the shifts. He could fix them before his lord noticed. He pulled Yorick past the brambles covered in snow, the thorns snagging their cloaks, and made it to the front doors of the tower without incident.

Unfortunately, the ward upon the front door was another matter. The magic power spiked as Yorick neared and Nezael drew him back before it struck. "Stay here," Nezael said. "I'll be out soon."

All Yorick could do was nod and Nezael didn't wait for it before he plunged through the ward himself and entered the tower.

"Bellamy!" Nezael called out and immediately turned for the nearest spiral stairwell to get to the armory room down below.

"Yes? Wait—" Bellamy's bones shambled as he ran after Nezael. He lumbered down the stairs after him. "Who is that outside? My little lord—"

"My friend." Nezael flung his magic through the armory to light the candles along the wall. The room had weapons bespelled by his lord and magical instruments carefully kept in cabinets along the walls. Nezael hurried to the nearest one and flung the doors open. Not what he needed. He closed it and went to the next one and then the next. Bellamy was on his heels in seconds and took Nezael's wrist, pulling him back.

"Nezael!" Bellamy snapped and hearing his name from Bellamy's skull made Nezael jump. "You brought an outsider here?"

Nezael frowned. "He's hardly an outsider," he insisted. "I'll fix the wards I pulled him through later."

"You've known him scarcely a *season*," Bellamy stressed. "You don't know him—"

"Too late for this conversation," Nezael cut him off. "Look, let my wrist go first." Magic coursed along Nezael's skin and Bellamy quickly let go before it licked his bones. "There is a beast terrorizing the town we use for supplies. Though I know our lord doesn't quite like how close it is, the town is a valuable asset. I told the man out there I'd help find the maligned beast." He plunged his hand into the cabinet and took the quartz amulet he spied within. It sparkled in the candlelight, magic swirling within its center. He threw it over his neck and turned for the weapons. "Our lord will never know."

Bellamy didn't answer right away. He stiffly watched Nezael, silent as a statue.

"Bellamy," Nezael whispered and touched his hand gently. "Trust me."

A resigned sigh trickled out of Bellamy's skull. "I do," he said. "But I feel this will prove badly for you." He squeezed his fingers around Nezael's, comforting. "Any beast prowling during the winter is dangerous, no matter if it has magic or not. Be careful."

"I always am."

He even made sure to grab the spelled axe for Yorick. It was heavy—Nezael needed help getting it up the stairs—but Yorick held it with such ease, it felt like he was showing off.

"Just in case," Nezael said. "Now, show me where the beast was when the town saw it." He held up his amulet. "I can track it with this."

The trek to town was smooth once they'd found the trail. The snow had been tramped down already by other travelers and a few mingled outside on the way. More of them than not eyed Nezael curiously as he trailed closely after Yorick, but they never asked who he was even if it was clear they warmly recognized Yorick. It was different than at the market, but Nezael forced himself to focus. He was doing a good deed and they would see that, suspicion or not.

Yorick took him to the bridge into town where the holly plants still hung. Everyone stayed clear of it today. Some of the holly had been torn down, trampled by what appeared to be a paw in the dirt.

"I was told the beast couldn't go any farther than this," Yorick said. "Wouldn't go over running water either, but it's got people spooked."

Nezael's heart jolted as his gaze darted across the holly bundles. It was the ones he'd enchanted keeping the beast at bay. His blood chilled, thinking of the town being gone if he hadn't thought to touch them. He bent low and felt the trampled ones with bare fingers. There was magic atop it lingering from the beast. Except it felt like his lord's. Like the doe. Of course. The stench was even the same, rotting yes, but also a sear of magic in the air.

Yorick bent beside him, bringing with him an entirely better aroma of cloves wafting off his clothes, and he watched Nezael expectantly.

"It *is* like the doe," Nezael whispered. "When my lord wakes, I'll have him learn why his magic is leaking out like this. For now..." He pulled the quartz amulet from his neck and held it above the crushed holly. With his free hand, he drew a finger into the dirt to make a glyph around the paw print.

The necklace froze at once, magic threads snagging it still from the glyph. He focused power into it and shushed Yorick when he opened his mouth with an inane question that would be answered shortly.

Nezael blocked everything out but the quartz and the presence of rotting, corrupted magic. The land grew dark and gray around him, leaving only the paw prints obscured with snow, and he was led to a place unseen in the distance. He drew his focus tighter, letting it take away his vision, and magic guided him along the path through the bloodied snow. It weaved in and out of trees until it found the beast's den in a small cave against a hill. It was deep in the forest, surrounded by brambles and thorns, but also spruces on almost all sides. Secluded.

The magic pushed him into the darkness of the den and lit up around the mangled beast, haloing its head with light. It was hunched over, fur splitting as magic sought to strengthen the bones and muscle within. Nezael looked around the beast, where it had laid the meager food it managed to catch, and his stomach dropped. There were three smaller beasts, emaciated and dead. Their bodies too weak to withstand whatever the magic was doing.

Suddenly, the beast gazed up and Nezael closed the connection. He flew back to himself, to Yorick, and drew in a sudden shuddering breath as his vision returned. The chill prickled its way down his throat, making him cough.

"I saw it," Nezael whispered as Yorick rubbed his back. "It's in a cave near a hill—deep in the forest. Where are there hills?"

Yorick's eyebrows went up. "I know where some are," he said and helped Nezael to his feet. The magic had left Nezael's legs weak and he was surprised when he had to hold onto Yorick's arm for balance. "We can make it before it grows dark. Follow me."

~

YORICK'S STRIDES WERE LONG, CARVING THROUGH THE

snow with ease, and it was all Nezael could do to keep up. His speed helped, at the very least. Day would quickly turn to dusk and then night would approach if they weren't careful. If it became too dark and they were still out in the woods? It wouldn't end well for either of them even *with* magic.

This deep into the woods, everything was hushed against the fallen snow. There was no sound but their own as they trudged on through into places hardly anyone had tread in years if Nezael had to guess. Pines stood tall with snow covered branches, protecting the ground below it from much of the snowfall, and their trail began to even out as a result. Yorick's path followed what Nezael had seen with magic and as they drew ever closer, Nezael took Yorick's arm to slow him down. If the beast was near, Nezael didn't want to frighten it.

They stopped at a rather large tree and peered around it. There was the shallow cave as Nezael had seen in the vision. Blood stained the snow outside, some of it still twisting with magic, turning into little spikes. Desecrated corpses lay dead and mangled, some whole, others with pieces of their bodies outright missing. Travelers left here to die because of a beast mad with magic. There was nothing Nezael could do for them now. There was shuffling deep in the dark, pained moans and cries, and Nezael drew back against Yorick.

"Plan?" Yorick asked, gripping the axe tight.

"I need to see it," Nezael said. "Find out why this happened."

Yorick breathed out. "So, into the den?"

"Yes," Nezael said slowly, hating the plan as much as

Yorick must have. "If we can draw it out, I can bind it." He mentally turned over the glyph he was thinking of in his head. Not complicated, but he needed time. "I'll draw the ward on the ground and you lure it over."

"Understood."

Before Yorick headed forth, Nezael brought him down for a quick kiss. "For luck," he said and delighted in the way Yorick smiled before he kissed him back.

Yorick slipped around the tree and Nezael hurried forward to begin the glyph. The dirt was clear, the thick branches crisscrossing overhead preventing the snow from obscuring it, and he held the quartz amulet in the air until it floated, suspended on its magic alone. Yorick delved into the den, bravery keeping his shoulders straight, and before long, a roar rumbled out.

Nezael shot magic into the quartz, making it light up like the sun, and out came threads like spears following his finger. Quickly, he drew one quarter of the glyph and the spears responded in kind on the other sides. It worked just as his lord had showed him and before Nezael could admire his handiwork, Yorick was coming back, sprinting. Nezael pushed magic toward Yorick, gripping him, and yanked him out of the beast's on-coming swipe. The force sent Yorick flying past Nezael, but he was safe, and Nezael withdrew after him.

The beast was large, wolf-like, but any resemblance to the creature was lost with what magic had done to it. Teeth too long to close its mouth and grown sharpened beyond need, its skin had split along its back to make room for the spine protruding from its skin as rows of spikes, and claws protruded from paws too small to accommodate them. Wherever the skin had split, the fur was matted with blood. Its eyes burned like brimstone, bright and wild, and set a hateful gaze on Nezael.

A beastly cry spilled out of its unhinged jaw, loud enough to shake everything around them. Nezael held his ground and willed the ward to rise. It struggled as the ground trembled from the beast's oncoming stomps, and just as the beast opened its maw, shadowing Nezael entirely, Yorick gripped him across the chest and lurched backwards.

The beast missed, swallowing nothing but air, and Nezael tightened his hold on the ward even as he and Yorick went tumbling. The edge finally rose, passing through the beast and stopped it in its tracks with a sickening crunch against its bones. The poor thing wailed in pain, thrashing, until the ward only tightened its grip.

"Are you unhurt?" Nezael breathed, trying to quell his racing heart.

Yorick swallowed and nodded. "You shot me into brambles, but I'm fine."

At least they were both safe and that was what mattered. Nezael stood, indicating for Yorick to stay there, and carefully approached the beast. It whined, blood dripping from the open sores along its back, and Nezael studied the magic.

It was indeed his lord's. All of it. He frowned. It was wrong. Driving the poor beast mad with pain.

"Well?" Yorick had dared to come closer, out of breath still. "Can you help it?"

"No," Nezael whispered. "Not with magic in its bones like that. This... this is wrong." Bile rose in his throat. "It's manipulating the bones while it's still alive—this is torture." His lord must have wanted beasts for his plans. What better way than tempt poor animals who didn't know better to eat something enchanted with magic such as this? It'd break down their skin and minds from the inside out until the bones broke out of their own will. If his lord could tame such a beast, he'd have more fodder for his army.

The ward audibly cracked. Nezael's jaw dropped, eyes wide, and Yorick threw himself into Nezael just as the beast lunged. Nezael ripped the magic out of the ward and fashioned it into a shield around them before the jaws came snapping down. The beast rebounded off the magic, blown back toward its den, and gave them room. Yorick hopped to his feet, axe in hand, and the beast came again. Yorick pivoted, leading it away from Nezael, but he needed help. Nezael snatched the quartz amulet from the ground and used it as a focus. He slammed it into the dirt, willing magic to move, and it ruptured the very earth in front of him. The beast's leg came down in the earth, crunching in half, and it howled in pain as its entire body slumped. Nezael drew the earth tighter, forgone apologies on his lips, and kept it there.

"Strike it!" Nezael shouted.

But the beast yanked its entire leg off. Nezael froze, panicked, and it lunged for Yorick before he was ready. The world went slow as Yorick fell backwards with a misplaced dodge, and the beast descended on him, sharp teeth gleaming. Then, it all sped up, power coursing through Nezael's body as he drew magic from the air. It froze the beast mid-lunge, its mighty jaw a hair's breadth away from Yorick's neck, and Nezael held it as tight as possible.

"Now!" he shouted again. "Strike it now!"

Yorick threw himself back to his feet and the axe's blade sung through the air as it came down. The spell across the metal kept it going and it cleaved through the poor beast's neck in one swoop. Nezael only released his magic when the head thumped to the ground, no life left in its brimstone eyes. The blood spilled forth from both sides, a nauseatingly bright red, and Nezael let go of the body entirely. It hit the ground with a rumble and only then did Nezael feel the tears on his cheeks.

His legs folded beneath him and he sank to the earth, unable to draw any real deep breath. They were ragged and panicked, his pulse pounding loud in his ears. The doe had been a docile creature. She hadn't been like this even at her worst. This mighty beast laid low all because his lord's magic pulled it apart. And for what? An ignoble death trying to protect its rotting offspring deep in the cave, already succumbed to the same magic. What had his lord hoped to achieve? The questions spun, echoing in Nezael's head, until Yorick was there, hands pressed to his face to make him look up.

"Nezael?" he whispered, like he'd already repeated it a few times before. "Are you unhurt still?"

Nezael nodded, trying to rid himself of the what ifs. "Yes. Are you? I'm sorry my ward was weak."

Yorick winced as he helped Nezael up. "I'm fine."

Nezael's gaze shot to his shoulder. He hadn't noticed the blood seeping through the fabric or the gouges deep in the skin underneath. "No, the beast harmed you." He pushed Yorick's hand off when he tried to stop him and peered at it closer. No magic he could detect, but grisly all the same.

He let out a relieved breath and rested his forehead against Yorick's chest. "I think it should be fine until we return to your cabin. No magic got inside it."

"It hurts like hell, but I'll live," Yorick whispered. "I'm alive. You're alive." He gently drew a hand through Nezael's hair.

More tears slipped down Nezael's cheeks. "It wanted food," he whispered. "Only magic had already rotted away its offspring. If it'd been weaker, it would have died with them. I just... I don't know what my lord's magic was doing beyond carving bone from skin. this... this was monstrous."

There wasn't an answer and Nezael had no idea how he'd even ask his lord. He wasn't even supposed to be outside, let alone this far. Never supposed to question him. He struggled on anything else to say and ceased trying altogether when Yorick kissed his forehead.

"We can come back tomorrow to deal with the bodies," he said and Nezael nodded against him. "We both need rest."

The adrenaline had run its course, washing right out of Nezael's body, and he trembled all the way back to the cabin. Yorick, thankfully, remained as sturdy as ever even though he winced every time he moved the wounded shoulder. They reached his cabin as the sky streaked with the golds and oranges of dusk and Nezael hurried him inside so he could look at the wound.

Not too deep, but needed stitching to keep the skin

together. Nezael was glad Isabella had shown him how to do so numerous times, insisting she wanted him to be prepared for anything. It wasn't like Carrow had shown Nezael how to heal with magic yet.

Nezael had Yorick sit in his kitchen as he maneuvered around to find herbs to use, water to wash out the wound, and a needle and thread to tie it all back together. The wound washed out quickly, magic making it faster, and as it worked, Nezael made a paste from the herbs. His hands were gentle and quick, the stitching as neat as he could make it, and he left kisses after each one. Then went on the poultice, pressed against the wound with a strip of cloth to hold it there.

Once that was taken care of, Nezael checked the rest of Yorick. Bruises colored his skin, but nothing as serious as the shoulder. Good. As Nezael attempted to go to the sink to wash the rags he'd used for cleaning, Yorick drew him suddenly close until he was practically straddling Yorick's lap.

"Thank you," Yorick said into Nezael's neck. He kissed it gently and Nezael drew his fingers through Yorick's hair soothingly. "If you hadn't helped, I don't think I would have been able to do it."

Nezael distantly realized Yorick would have died on his own and the thought made him cold.

"I was glad to help." Nezael kissed Yorick's head and then lower to his mouth for a deeper one. Yorick's hand firmly kept him there until they both mutually had to part. "Rest," Nezael said and slid off Yorick's lap. "I'll return tomorrow with something for the pain."

"I'll see you tomorrow, then."

Yorick smiled at him and Nezael knew then and there, this was all worth it. Damn Bellamy's worry and whatever his lord might think. Doing this meant something and being here like this was more than the tower had ever given him. Real purpose beyond a vague taking the world back. His lord likely didn't even know what that meant at this point.

After another chaste kiss, Nezael was out the door and into the blooming twilight to hurry home.

SEVEN
ARISE

A ND SO, ON AND ON WINTER WENT. NOT ALWAYS AS exciting as the beast in the hill, but Nezael found comfort in that nothing like that happened again. He continued visiting Yorick and—much to his own shock—they didn't end up naked in bed together every time. Nezael learned various card games from Yorick that he gleefully taught Bellamy to pass the time. He tried to bring Bellamy to the cabin many times so the three of them could play, but the skeleton was insistent *someone* had to watch the tower. Yorick himself wouldn't come to the tower again, saying it felt wrong even being there. No matter. Nezael happily spread his time between the two places. He even began trekking his spell book back and forth and soon, Yorick became a good sounding board for the magic spells Nezael was penning. Sure, Yorick never understood the nuances or exactly how it worked, but having someone who happily listened and wouldn't interrupt him like Bellamy was nice.

It felt too soon when winter began to thaw and early spring flowers bloomed defiant against the frost. Birds returned to the woods, singing their morning songs, and Nezael's own skeleton bird joined them with its own bone rattle cadence.

Nezael dressed lighter today, glad for the less frigid air, and as he headed down the tower to meet up with Yorick, Bellamy caught him before he left.

"You know what day it is, yes?" Bellamy asked.

Nezael hesitated. It couldn't be. "I thought there were a few more days."

"Tonight, everyone will wake by your hand. You must be back before dark. Yes, yes. I know you always are," Bellamy interrupted Nezael's thought before he voiced it. "But be back *sooner*. It takes time rousing everyone and you know it."

"Of course I will be." Nezael straightened his cloak and smiled. "I've a mind to trudge to town to get one of those spring cakes for our lord. You know how he loves them so."

Bellamy didn't look quite convinced that it had been Nezael's plan all along—it certainly wasn't—but he wasn't outright lying. Nezael *had* intended to purchase the cakes eventually, he just hadn't thought it'd be so soon. Carrow always brought cakes when he roused the skeletons to reward Nezael for another year together. Nezael figured he could do it too.

And Nezael brightened realizing he didn't have to do it alone. He had a helper in mind and it would be remiss of him to not properly thank his helper. He just didn't want to tell Bellamy that. Finally, Bellamy released a low sigh, and patted Nezael's cheek.

"See to it then, little lord," he said. "Be back before dusk."

"I will."

~

A REWARD WAS STILL A REWARD, EVEN IF IT WAS GIVEN first, right? And it was given so all-encompassing and rigorously, Nezael forgot all about the task at hand, lost in Yorick entirely. Until he roused from an afterglow nap and saw how low the sun was. Then all his plans came back in a rush and he swore, shooting upright on his elbows. The motion jostled Yorick below him and he winced.

"I forgot the cakes," he breathed.

Yorick made a sleepy sound of his own, blinking blearily, and drew his hand down the curve of Nezael's back, tracing his skin gently like it would coax him back down.

"Your pillow talk is usually about magic," Yorick said, drawing Nezael closer even as he tried to untangle himself from Yorick and the sheets. It was almost a useless effort, especially when Yorick's mouth found his shoulder and happily kissed it all the way up to his neck. "What's this about cakes?"

Nezael resisted Yorick's charms and shoved a pillow at him, making him laugh, and Nezael took his chance to crawl over Yorick to get to the edge of the bed. "My lord is waking tonight. I was going to get those spring cakes from town to celebrate." He wrinkled his nose as he drew his gaze across the dim cabin. "Yorick, why do you always throw my clothes *so* far?"

Yorick grinned mischievously at him as he put his hands behind his head. "So I can watch you go get them." He laughed again as Nezael threw the blanket over his head and hurried for his underclothes before Yorick recovered.

He'd just gotten them yanked on when Yorick spoke again, his voice meeker this time without any of the teasing.

"Your lord's waking tonight?"

Even Nezael heard the unease and tried to ignore it as he glanced back at Yorick. The man wasn't quite looking up at him like he feared the answer.

"Yes," Nezael said, sad for the drastic shift in mood. He spotted his leggings over the counter and went to retrieve them. Right, he'd barely gotten in the door before Yorick was upon him and yanking off articles of clothing. "Usually, we'd use this day to rouse the skeletons together, but this time, he needs rousing." He fastened them and found his shirt on the table. There was a small exhale from Yorick and Nezael peered over as he threw the shirt on. "Is something wrong?"

Yorick had found his own pants and was pulling them on too. No show for Nezael this time. "Nothing, just thinking too hard." Yorick stood and buttoned his pants. "You'll still be able to come by?"

"Of course." Nezael came back and was delighted when Yorick reached out and pressed him as close as they could get. Though Nezael kissed him softly, Yorick leaned in deeper, one hand entangled in Nezael's hair to keep him there and that left the other wandering down the small of Nezael's back to squeeze Nezael's behind. The kiss ended with Nezael giggling. "You can't tempt me back into bed." He wiggled out of Yorick's hands. "Help me find the cakes? The baker loves you more than me."

"You know I will."

~

THE TOWN WAS MUCH MORE ALIVE AS THE SNOW MELTED from its streets. Few outdoor market stalls were open this early in the season, plying crafts made over the long winter. There was an energy here the place had been lacking throughout the winter and for once, Nezael appreciated it. The world was coming alive again.

Like he thought, the baker *loved* Yorick, but the man also remembered Nezael from before when he came once with Agatha. That was enough to get a warm hello and Nezael was flustered until Yorick and the baker got to talking about what he'd been making.

Spring cakes were always made this time each year. Old ingredients left over from hunkering down in the winter and seasoned with berries only found at the start of spring. The baker parted with four and carefully arranged them together so they would not be mashed by the time Nezael got back to the tower. They smelled so divine, Nezael had to resist sharing them immediately with Yorick. Maybe another time.

They made their leave and rejoined the cold breeze rustling through town. Yorick hurried Nezael through the dwindling streets so close to dusk and up the trail leading to the brambles and thorns the wards were made around. Nezael had strengthened them the week before and no longer could Yorick pass through them on his own. It had to remain this way.

Before Nezael could say goodbye, Yorick had pushed him up to a tree for a deep kiss. Nezael lingered for as long as he dared, entangled within Yorick. They parted breathless too soon and Yorick rested his forehead against Nezael's.

"You're acting like I'll be gone forever," Nezael said.

"I know you won't be, but now you'll have other duties too and I'll have to share you." Yorick's blue eyes were twinkling from the way the sun set around the forest. "Promise me you'll come down like you used to. We can find spring herbs together."

"I will forevermore." Nezael softly kissed Yorick and drew back before it could go any farther. "I might even have a skeleton in tow."

"I'd love to meet them." Yorick released Nezael from the tree and squeezed his hand. "See you soon, then?"

Nezael smiled at him, all warm and tingly inside. "Soon, I promise." He kissed Yorick's knuckles gently and loved the way it made Yorick's lips stretch in a soft smile.

With a gentle wave, Nezael stepped through the ward. It obscured Yorick on the other side where all Nezael could see was the shape of his body. No doubt to Yorick, Nezael would have simply disappeared into the brambles and thorns. He lingered until Yorick's form turned away and then he hurried on his way. No more dallying; he had his lord to rouse this night.

Upon his return, Bellamy didn't bother to hide his exasperation from how close Nezael was cutting it, and he immediately got to work. First, he set up the dining hall with the cakes and took care in choosing one of his lord's wines to start the year right. It would have been nice to share a bottle with Yorick, now that Nezael thought about it, but as soon as the idea surfaced, he shook it away. *Focus*, he told himself.

Bellamy had taken it upon himself to find the enchanted decanter for the rousing potion and Nezael gathered the life blossoms from Isabella's stores. She was the first to be roused, as always. Bellamy assisted, unwrapping her bones delicately, and Nezael crushed a life blossom before mixing it with a cup of rousing potion. He tipped it gently into her skull and it never spilled out. Instead, like magic, the mixture poured into her very bones to reinvigorate what magic was stored within. Lastly, with a magic upon his breath, Nezael breathed into Isabella. The skeleton's magic awoke, filling her with life stored away during the winter.

The process wasn't hard and Nezael had seen it first-hand so many times assisting his lord, but he'd forgotten just how many skeletons there were. Many he couldn't remember the names of alongside the few of his inner circle who exclusively cared for him. His magic renewed them all, just like Carrow's had done before, but Nezael's own body began to tremble in response from an over-taxing of magic. His vision waned with each new breath, pain wound its way through every inch of his body as he forced his magic to work, and all he wanted to do was rest. Except he couldn't. He forced himself to stay awake, deal with the pain.

By the time he made it upward to his lord, last as Bellamy had dictated, he was shaking so much, Bellamy had to help him up the steps.

"It'll be fine, my little lord," Bellamy whispered as he drew a reassuring hand through Nezael's hair. The tower below was alive with the activity of skeletons returning to their posts and preparing the place for their true lord's awakening. "The first time is always hard."

Nezael paused at Carrow's door. "How many first times have you seen?"

Bellamy didn't answer and the silence thickened the air between them. He wouldn't even look down at Nezael before he took Nezael's hand and pushed it to the ward in the door. The glyphs on the surface began to turn like a wheel, the outer ones started first one way, and then the next section the other way, until they were all turning. Eventually, they began dissipating one by one and the magic entered Nezael's arm as power. Thick and true, it shot pain through his arm and made his vision blur with bright spots. He wanted to draw his hand away, but Bellamy held it there until the ward was no more.

Nezael steeled himself with a deep breath and pushed the door open. The woven spells and wards snapped as he came through alone. Magic parted like curtains, revealing the sleeping form of his lord.

Exactly as Nezael had left him months ago.

The same handsome face softened with blissful sleep. Carrow hadn't aged and nor had he changed one bit. It almost reminded Nezael of a sleeping prince, but what Carrow could be the prince of wouldn't come. Then, there was a soft thought like a whisper to leave him there. Did he truly need Carrow? Nezael dashed it aside as soon as it emerged and shook his head. Without

Carrow, Nezael wouldn't be here—he was sure of it. That was that.

"I am here, my lord," Nezael whispered, lowering himself at his lord's side.

He crushed the life blossom in his palm and mixed it into the decanter itself to dissolve. The liquid took on a spectral hue, shining like a prism as Nezael swirled it, and he poured as much as he could into his own mouth. Magic collected there, bright and warm from his own throat as a spell, and Nezael reached over to press his lips to Carrow's. As the spell required, the waking draught flowed from Nezael and into his lord, tingling his lips with warmth as it went.

And that was it. Nezael's legs folded beneath him, leaving him on the floor with no strength left to give, but he didn't outright fall. Carrow had caught him and drew him close. His opened eyes twinkled like firelight as magic hummed across him. He brushed Nezael's hair back with his hand, smiling.

"Oh, my blossom," Carrow whispered and Nezael's body shivered hearing his deep voice again after months of silence. "I didn't think this would be so hard on you."

"Good morning," Nezael tried, but his voice was a soft sigh mimicking words. His body couldn't hold him up and he stopped trying. He was content there across his lord's lap, he was sure, but then Carrow stood like he'd never been asleep. Magic traced the air after him, threads trailing from him to the bed, and each one brushed up against Nezael as they snapped to let Carrow go. His lord bent low, gently gathering Nezael into his arms, and with no effort, lifted him off the floor.

Carrow's touch was incredibly gentle, his voice soft against Nezael even though Nezael couldn't for the life of him remember what Carrow had said, and between blinks, Nezael was in his own bed, changed into sleeping clothes and covered in blankets.

"Rest, my blossom." Carrow kissed Nezael's hand and left it over the edge of the blanket. "You have done enough." With careful fingers, he pulled the chain of the necklace he'd given Nezael months ago over his head. Magic sparkled as it went. Nezael reached for it sleepily, but Carrow caught the hand and kissed it again.

"*Sleep*," Carrow insisted, his gaze never straying from Nezael's. His eyes were so mesmerizing. The twinkling amber with a golden halo of magic glowing in the irises. The necklace disappeared into Carrow's coat and Nezael's eyelids began to fall.

"I will wake you anon, but you must rest and recover." Magic followed Carrow's voice, gently settling across Nezael as yet another blanket. Once it had settled, Carrow leaned over Nezael and kissed him on the forehead.

And that was it. Sleep dragged Nezael under as ordered and magic tingled across his entire body. It fluttered up and down, reminiscent of kisses, and all Nezael dreamed of was Yorick himself chasing the sensation. Up and down Nezael's skin like he'd done so many times before.

EIGHT

NECROMANCER

NEZAEL AWOKE TO GOLDEN SUNSHINE PEERING through his windows. It cast a shimmering hue across his entire room and he felt revitalized beneath its light. Magic hummed through his veins anew, soothing the exhaustion from last night, and he was just so *warm*. He made to close his eyes again, relish in spring's first rays of dawn, when he noticed Bellamy watching him from his desk. All sleep snapped away in an instant, reality reminding him of last night and how he'd roused everyone from slumber, and Nezael propped himself up on his elbows. Bellamy merely watched him, turning over a silver chain in his hand. Around and around it went almost rhythmically, until he came to the end of the chain where the charm of a looking glass lay. Then he began turning it anew. Nezael felt his throat, finding his own gone. Right. His lord had taken the necklace.

"Good morning," Nezael said and Bellamy twitched as though he hadn't noticed Nezael awake. "Is something the matter?"

A soft sigh resounded from Bellamy's skull and he stopped turning the chain over in his hand. "Our lord wishes your presence in the great hall as soon as you wake. As such, I was sent here to await you." He turned and slid a plate toward Nezael from the other side of the desk. A simple helping of eggs and sausage, all seasoned with Agatha's usual flair. "Agatha sent me with food."

Nezael took the plate, stomach growling fiercely, and sat cross legged in bed to eat. Yep, Definitely Agatha's. He'd missed it so much. His and Bellamy's breakfasts could never compare. Maybe he could sneak her to Yorick's cabin and they could cook together. He'd like to see it. Both of them side-by-side as they traded dish ideas back and forth. It'd be sweet.

The silence in his room, however, dug into him, and he glanced up at Bellamy again. The skeleton was still staring. Distant.

"Are you well, Bellamy?" Nezael tried, worry squeezing him tight.

"Our lord has found you a skeleton."

Excitement shot through Nezael and he almost threw his plate aside with his blankets. "So soon?"

"Our lord wished not to delay."

Bellamy's voice was so muted and cold, it stole the excitement out of Nezael. He gently placed his half-eaten breakfast on the desk and reached out to touch Bellamy's hand. Magic glinted off the chain upon his touch, and with a puff, it exhaled and was gone.

"What aren't you telling me?" he tried.

Bellamy never once looked away until now. "Everything will be fine." He slid the necklace into his jacket, leaving it out of sight, and straightened his lapels. "Remember that no matter what, my little lord."

Nezael looked up at the skeleton. "Why do you have my necklace?"

"Lord Carrow has finished with it and saw fit to have me hold onto it." Bellamy beckoned Nezael up and revealed the garments behind him. "He also weaved you your own necromancer robes. Please, get dressed and meet him downstairs. He expects you any moment now."

There was urgency in Bellamy's voice and though Nezael wanted to take time to admire his new garments, he hurried for Bellamy's sake. The tunic was in muted red tones and wrapped snug around his body and had a black cowl holding onto a large hood. Gloves went up the length of his arm and tightened near the top with magic gems sewn along the insides. Bellamy helped affix the ornamental golden spine to the back, along Nezael's own spine, and magic ghosted across it once Bellamy folded the rib pieces against Nezael's torso. Magic armor—it would stop blows so long as it remained enchanted. The gold shimmered and Nezael liked the skeleton motif. The last to go on beyond simple dark leggings and boots was a black sash dusted in silver like stardust. It resembled the one his lord wore.

"There now," Bellamy breathed. "Our little lord is now our little necromancer." It felt like he smiled as he reached out to squeeze Nezael's shoulder. "See to our lord now. No more distractions."

Nezael wanted to feel ecstatic. His lord saw fit to weave him his own necromancer robes and he was getting a skeleton of his own this day. Yet Bellamy's voice chilled him all the way through. This was not a happy occasion and Nezael couldn't figure out *why*.

Perhaps Bellamy himself was tired. He walked stiffer as they left Nezael's room. Yes. That had to be it. It made sense. He'd been up all winter, after all. Believing it eased the fear and Nezael hurried through the tower by himself. It teemed with renewed magic, thick on the air, and Nezael could practically taste it.

The skeleton—*his* skeleton—awaited and he'd make it wait no longer.

The tower's main thoroughfare was cold. Someone had left the door propped open. Golden light spilled in and no one sought to close it as the tower aired out. Footprints tracked in from outside to the great hall at the very end and though fear prickled Nezael's insides, he pushed it down. His lord was careful when he made skeletons. Surely, this was no different.

He entered the hall, slipping through the crack in the door left open for him, and all the warmth fled his body. There was blood *everywhere*, but most of all concentrated in the long streak dragged from the door he'd slipped in through and up to the wooden plinth in the center. His breakfast came up fast, but he swallowed it down, forcing in a shaking breath. Skeletons were made from the dead. Blood was sometimes a byproduct.

His eyes tracked forward to the plinth, where his lord stood, arms up to the elbows dripping in blood, staining the white shirt he wore. There was a smile on his lips, but it held no warmth, even when he trained it on Nezael. Near him were tables clearly rolled in from elsewhere given how mismatched they felt to everything around them. Atop them were stone trays and Nezael had to swallow down his breakfast a second time seeing what was upon them. Organs were potent ingredients, his lord had always said, and there they were. Slick with blood still dripping down the sides.

Nezael's gaze finally darted to the plinth and the body atop it.

"Come, come," Carrow invited. "Don't just stand there gawking."

Nezael hardly heard him over the racing of his pulse, but his legs lumbered forward so distantly from his own wants. His breathing became rapid, the cold air of the room snaking down his throat with each one, and it only worsened the closer he came to the body on the plinth. Tawny skin still mostly whole, but streaked with blood from incisions to extract the organs. Between his legs had been eviscerated, smeared in blood and gore where nothing else remained. Nezael's gaze traced up the body, his own shivering in fear, and he ignored everything he knew. Everything he'd touched with lips and hands both, until he came to the face.

The whole world became distant and gone in an instant. Silent, save for the sound of his pulse.

Because it was Yorick laying on the plinth.

The sound Nezael made was not one he could ever repeat. A strangled gasp of terror, revulsion, and panic all but smothered beneath his hand.

"You're not too late, my blossom," Carrow said. "Your skeleton is still there. I merely started the process because I know excavation is hard at first." He traced a bloody finger down the chest already carved open. The chest Nezael had traced with his fingers and lips both just yesterday.

"Where—" Nezael swallowed back a retch. "Where'd you find him?"

Carrow tilted his head toward Nezael, eyes wide with delight. "Oh, the first thing I should have told you about skeletons is that your first one is made easier if it's someone you already love." He paused, watching Nezael, and all Nezael could do was freeze under his lord's stare. "Bellamy was like a brother to me. When he fell, it was only natural I raise him as my first because I could not bear to leave him in the dirt."

"H-He wasn't dead," Nezael whispered.

Carrow shrugged. "Humans are incredibly fragile creatures." His gaze drifted to Yorick's legs and Nezael couldn't look. Not again. "Oh, my blossom. My blossom." He came over and turned Nezael's chin to face him. His hands were cold and slick with blood. "I thought you'd be *happy*. Why are you so sad? I found you a skeleton."

Why was he sad? Yorick was cold. Yorick's lips were pale. Yorick's blue eyes were already gone on a tray, blood running down his cheeks from the holes left behind. His once vibrant hair lay slack, crowning his head with dried blood clumped between the strands. He'd never speak with his own voice again. His laugh would change. Every bit of him all but gone except for the skeleton within. A life torn apart and discarded because of Nezael. All because of him.

It made tears fall. Made every part of Nezael numb with horror.

"Come now," Carrow whispered as he wiped the tears with his thumb. "I'll help you." His lips pressed to Nezael's jaw softly. "I promise."

Detaching himself from his body didn't work, but Nezael still felt outside himself as Carrow led him to the other side of the plinth. Every step was real. Right there. But unreal at the same time, like his body couldn't decide if it was. The first thing he had to do to connect himself to the skeleton—to Yorick—was to connect himself to the heart. The once core of a human from where blood flowed into it and out of it to make the body function. He had to eat it. Let his magic absorb it.

It was soft as Nezael's teeth pierced it. As what blood remained inside gushed into his mouth and down his chin. The way it ran down between his fingers as he held it there. Each time he swallowed, his lord pressed a lingering kiss to his throat. Nezael didn't know how long it took or how many times he almost retched it back up only to find Carrow's hand at his back to coax it back down. Only, it was done. His vision blurred, staring down at Yorick. Feeling his heart in his chest. Whether it was his or not, he didn't know. Only it was there. Apparent and loud.

Carrow slowly cleaned off Nezael's fingers, lips cold against each one.

"There," Carrow murmured. "It wasn't so hard now, was it?" He angled Nezael's head toward him, his eyes alight with bright magic that flickered, and he pressed his lips to Nezael's.

The kiss was nothing soft or comforting. Hunger descended on Nezael's mouth, holding him so tight in its grip, Nezael couldn't fight it. All he tasted was blood. All he felt was his lord's tongue as it tasted all Nezael ever was as though reclaiming him until Nezael was empty. Hollow. When Carrow finally drew away, it was with a self-satisfied smirk with lips smeared in blood.

"Let me show you now how to free his bones from within."

The skin pulled back beneath Nezael's fingers with the aid of a tool Nezael didn't bother to memorize or take note of. Blood ran down the plinth, clumping to the floor where Carrow liberally dropped tissue and muscle he hacked through to get to the bones within. The room smelled so starkly of death, of nothing remotely close to life like nothing had ever been alive there to begin with. The bones were extracted like it was a dream, each one with careful and precise movements to preserve what they were, and cleaned with rosewater and cedar oil. Yorick was beautiful beneath as he was on the outside, but Nezael hated this. Nothing was right. It had to be a nightmare. It had to be.

But then why wasn't he waking?

He numbly arranged the skeleton as he'd learned to. Carrow helpfully removed what wasn't needed from his path until it was just Nezael, the plinth, and Yorick's skeleton atop it. Everything else would be scrubbed away, become part of the tower to augment the magic within. Nezael would never see Yorick's face again. The man would never smile teasingly or crinkle his nose. His once blue eyes were on a tray only to be part of a potion or worse.

When Carrow finished cleaning what wasn't needed, he returned to Nezael's side and gently put his hands at Nezael's shoulders. "And now," he whispered into his ear, "he's all yours, my blossom." He turned Nezael to look at him. "Do you remember?"

"Yes, my lord," Nezael whispered, his voice hardly audible.

Carrow's wicked smile softened into something reminiscent of pride and he pressed a chaste kiss to Nezael's lips. Quick and soft, nothing like the hunger from before. Then, he withdrew, magic ghosting the tables of organs to follow him out until Nezael was alone in a room where time had stalled.

The warm, golden light was a mockery as it came in from the skylights above and as it haloed the gardens coming alive for spring outside the windows. This flagrant loss of life was drenched in such an ethereal glow, it almost looked as though it should have been a wondrous affair. Not this. Anything but this.

And Nezael cried. The tears began silent, but then he sobbed, unable to hold it in and it only prompted more sobs to work their way out of his chest.

"I'm—I'm so sorry, Yorick—I—I—" He didn't know how to finish the thought. If Yorick could even hear him in his state. If his soul wasn't already gone—let go—and left Nezael to fail like he deserved. He *wanted* to fail, but if Yorick was still there, waiting or trapped, he couldn't leave his soul suspended there, could he?

"I'm so sorry."

It was all he could say. Yorick was dead. No words would bring him back the way he was.

There were three life blossoms twinkling on the plinth. The first one, Nezael gently kissed each petal and placed it within Yorick's mouth, deep in his skull. Another would become the core for his new heart, but the rest, crushed and mixed with Nezael's and Yorick's blood. The process made Nezael's vision sway as he drained his blood into the pestle, as he mixed it with what Carrow had left for him, and then came the crushed petals. Mix until it shimmered. And it did. A somber, golden light twinkling up at him.

With reverence, Nezael took each and every bone and coated them in the life blossom mixture and his magic both with a chant upon his lips to seal it. His voice was a muted echo through the room, oscillating with the latent magic until the very air buzzed. More tears came the closer Nezael came to prepping the core. They slipped from his cheeks to Yorick's. What Yorick had been. The Yorick stripped of everything beyond what had seeped down into his bones. They were coated and magicked now, the thin, unseen threads of magic pulling this way and that to create the muscles Nezael had once traced. The life blossom was bundled with the herbs he and Yorick had picked before winter drew them closer. It was almost funny; Yorick had chosen his own herbs with as much reverence as Nezael gave to his bones now.

It made him cry once more as he pressed his blood into the petals. He gently left it inside Yorick's ribs, his new heart suspended there with magic coiling around it.

And there it was: done and with it, the day's light

receded, leaving the room cold and gray, soft subtle blues ate away the gold as glinting magic began to form around Yorick's prone bones.

Nezael took a moment to recompose himself. Deep breaths as he wiped his tears, locking it all away until he felt absolutely nothing. It had to be this way now.

He needed air most of all. To look away from Yorick. He left the room, but couldn't go far because his lord was there in the hall. Nezael's body stiffened seeing him and the curious smile upon lips coated in dried blood.

"I'm finished," Nezael announced.

Yet he was too weak to resist as Carrow yanked his arm and braced Nezael up against the wall, fingers digging into his face to keep him still, and Nezael held his breath. Carrow's eyes remained bright with magic, never once dulling, and its power traced up and down his arm until Nezael felt it hold his body like a vice.

"Do you understand?" Carrow asked, anger pushing through each word as his voice dripped with magic. "That you are *no one* but my necromancer?" He ground Nezael's head into the wall, his hand shaking from holding his face so tightly.

Nezael shook his head and regretted it as Carrow's other hand snapped to his throat. "My-My lord!" he choked the words and felt tears slip out of his eyes again. "P-Please."

Carrow's fingers tightened, cutting off all other words. "I have no need for apprentices who think they are anything but." He pressed closer and Nezael could hardly draw in air. "You are mine and mine alone. Your mind, your body, everything you are and more. Do you understand me?"

Nodding was all Nezael could do and he did— anything to breathe again. Carrow released his hold so suddenly, Nezael would have collapsed to the floor if Carrow hadn't been there. As it was, after a few deep breaths against his lord's shoulder, Carrow pushed him back and kissed him again, stealing all air away. Magic lingered on Nezael's lips when he finally withdrew and let him sag against the wall.

"Good," Carrow whispered it so softly, it was like he'd never been angry, and he gently drew his hand through Nezael's hair. "Spend the night with what you've made and tomorrow morning, he will rise."

Carrow was barely out of view before Nezael's legs folded entirely, leaving him on the floor to sob behind the hands covering his mouth. He curled up as tight as he could to be as small as possible, and hide from the whole world. Until it slotted itself back together in something that made sense. Where Yorick was still alive and he'd never tempted fate by leaving the tower.

It never happened and nor was it long before he noticed a shadow next to him and he flinched. But it was only Bellamy. The skeleton knelt beside Nezael.

"Why?" Nezael choked out. "Why, Bellamy?"

"'Twas not my intent," he said sadly. He took the necklace from his jacket and let it hang in the space between them. A looking glass. Nezael's eyes widened as he gasped.

"It was enchanted to see me," he whispered.

Carrow had seen *everything*. Every touch. Every kiss. All Yorick had happily done to him and what Nezael had done in return. More tears raced down Nezael's cheeks and he covered his mouth to smother the scream clawing its way up his throat. Everything was his fault. If he hadn't left the tower... if he hadn't fallen for such a kind smile, Yorick would not be in there on the plinth. He'd be *alive*. Bellamy carefully drew Nezael closer and the smothered scream turned into sobs against his shoulder.

"I should have told you to run away with him," Bellamy whispered. "But if I lost another apprentice..." He sighed, the sound ghosting itself across Nezael's hair. "I valued my life more and I regret that I did. I am so, so sorry, my little lord."

He left Nezael there, but Nezael didn't have it in him to blame the skeleton. Nezael could have felt the magic upon the necklace all on his own and understood the implications of it around his own neck, but he'd simply been happy with a gift from the lord he trusted so completely. He should have opened his eyes sooner and saw the world for what it was. He watched Bellamy go and the way he still favored one leg as he limped. Not simple exhaustion, but magic deliberately stolen as punishment. Nezael breathed in, gathering a spell on his lips, and exhaled it.

Threads wove across the bones, strengthening them back together, and Bellamy walked straighter. He did not look back. He was Lord Carrow's skeleton, after all. He would never be Nezael's no matter how kind Nezael was.

But there was one skeleton primed to be wholly his and though Nezael wanted to run, never return, Yorick was *here*. Because of him. He couldn't leave the man he'd loved over the cold winter. Even if Yorick hated him when he awoke. Even if Yorick refused to wake. Whatever happened, happened. In any case, Nezael couldn't leave. His hands were tainted. He was Lord Carrow's necromancer.

And that was all he'd ever be, forevermore.

Yorick's skeleton lay there as still as death in the cold room. The herbs glowed against the magic threads woven around the bones and gave it a pleasant, soothing smell that washed away the stench of death. Almost like cloves and cinnamon. Nezael returned to the plinth, each limb trembling. The magic had created a gossamer shroud around Yorick, making him shimmer. Nezael laid himself inside the shroud and curled up around the skeleton of the man he'd touched so lovingly before.

"Yorick," he whispered, feeling the shroud shift with his voice. "I'm sorry. It wasn't supposed to be this way." He stroked the skull with his knuckles and wasn't sure why he waited for a response. He gently kissed it on the cheek and laid his head down beside it.

Because it would be a long night.

Even without the bliss of sleep, morning came. The dark had coated Nezael in a chill he couldn't shake, and then pale oranges and yellows bloomed into the room, chasing it all away. Before long, even the sun shined inside, golden and bright. Alive. And right there, Nezael felt the soul folded against his back like Yorick had done so many times in his own bed. Arms wrapped tight around Nezael as though he might lose him otherwise.

Nezael let the sensation linger for as long as he dared before he lifted his hand. The soul followed it, leaving the ghost of soft kisses along his fingers, and he wove it into the skeleton's heart. With a shimmer, Nezael's magic bloomed across the bones in earnest as the soul helped them connect to what was once its tissue and muscle. There was a sort of life there now, blazed anew by magic, and the bones trembled together like someone rousing from slumber.

Yorick sat up, wavering, and Nezael came up with him, a steady hand at his back. He never looked away once as Yorick stared at him, eye sockets empty of the blue eyes that used to be there. Yorick touched Nezael's cheek with his hand and Nezael held it there. Warm. It was warm.

"You are mine," Nezael whispered and magic sung softly across his words. "You are mine, Yorick, forevermore."

"I am yours, Nezael," Yorick whispered, his voice ringing clear. "Forevermore."

Even as the tears renewed and fell, Nezael leaned close and kiss the skull, perhaps for the last time in the privacy of the morning before he locked himself away until he felt nothing else. "And, in return," Nezael whispered, "I am yours, Yorick, forevermore."

EPILOGUE
Darkness At the Heart of My Love

THE FLUTTERING KISSES BECAME SOFTER AND SOFTER, up and down the length of Nezael's body. It did every night. He'd arc into the touch, wanting it closer. Wanting to feel the weight of the kisses against his skin, but it was always fleeting. They were gone. A reminder softening slowly over time and Nezael feared it becoming so soft, it became too fragile to recall. Already, memories hid behind the ethereal shroud in his mind, completely out of reach by the time morning light slid across his room.

Nezael awoke alone and let himself be for a moment, so still and silent, until he was sure. He rolled over to his back and ran his fingers through his hair. Spring and half of summer had dragged by. Each day, he found himself beside his lord to assist in the army he was still raising.

Lord Carrow's promise of change had failed. They were *still* in the decrepit tower as the summer winds blew back the soft spring air. Carrow had ceased making such promises again. Things took time, he insisted, and that was the last Nezael heard about any timeframe. Mercenaries came and went like the wind and the nights grew long when Carrow had Nezael entertain them as well. Many lingered longer than Nezael liked.

Days blurred together in the throes of pulling the dead apart. As they magicked bones into motion which had long since lost sight of their souls together. As the heat of his lord's lips tinged in blood found his own. Blood always rushed down his throat. Splashed across his skin. He tasted it on the hungry lips of his lord. Then, by the night's end, the skeleton awoke, its mind melded between both their magics.

Even now, Nezael still tasted blood against the burn left yesterday by Carrow's teeth on his lips. Nezael sighed and dropped his arms onto the blankets.

He wanted to return to when it was simple. When he watched his lord raise skeletons. When Carrow treated him not as something to be completely devoured, but as a devoted pupil. Even more, Nezael wished he was in that grove clearing again. Dreaming of the ways Yorick could touch him if he'd simply ask. Dreaming of Yorick's body. Nezael thought deep, trying to remember it. The way his body vibrated when he laughed. The crinkle in his nose when he smiled. The warmth of his skin against Nezael's. The sounds they made when pressed so tightly together.

The door to his chambers opened, drawing Nezael out of his fantasy, and he stopped short of slipping his hands beneath his blankets to release the tension. A skeleton dressed in a tunic and breeches strode inside. *His* skeleton. *His* Yorick. Magic fluttered across his bones like foregone kisses and it let Yorick's once heart beat against Nezael's own. It had taken getting used to, but Nezael found solace in it now. Especially because Yorick had distanced himself as the months went by. The heartbeat reminded Nezael that Yorick was still there, even when Yorick tried desperately not to be.

Like now: he hardly glanced at Nezael as he placed a tray of breakfast on the desk. Wouldn't turn as Nezael sat up, letting the blanket pool around his waist to reveal his pale skin beneath. Marks Yorick had left once upon a time gone.

Maybe they couldn't go back to the touches they'd had before, but Nezael wished Yorick would look at him again like he used to. He'd feel it, Nezael was sure, and it would make everything right.

But it wasn't to be.

"Good morning, master," Yorick said, the timber of his voice hollow in his skull.

Nezael scowled. "Carrow's been talking to you." He grabbed his robe from where it hung on his bed post and extracted himself from the bed. What was once a tease back in Yorick's cabin where he'd delight in the man's eyes roving across his naked flesh was a cold reminder Yorick would do no such thing again. Nezael tied the robe tightly.

"Don't call me master or lord or anything of the sort." He gently took Yorick's hand. The bones were covered in the colorful wraps Isabella shared with him and magicked with Nezael's own spells to keep his bones from breaking. Nezael kissed each knuckle as he gazed up at Yorick who still would not look at him. "I'm still Nezael. Don't let him convince you otherwise. Please."

Yorick hesitated. The other skeletons in the tower had accepted him like an old friend as soon as he was walking alongside Nezael. But nevertheless, Nezael and Yorick agreed to keep their short history a secret. Bellamy already knew and perhaps for that reason, it took him the longest to warm up to Yorick. Perhaps he blamed the man for changing Nezael so. No longer a little lord kept protected, but now a willing participant to every nefarious or otherwise plan their lord deigned to give.

Agatha adored her new helper in the kitchen and alone with her, Yorick acted like his old self. A warm man relishing in ways to make her laugh. Isabella enjoyed a go-for that wasn't Nezael, but Nezael still took every opportunity he could to leave the tower in search of herbs with Yorick. Just to pretend winter hadn't ever ended. Even if Yorick was now a skeleton.

"I'm sorry," Yorick murmured and brought Nezael's hand to his mouth. No lips, but Nezael remembered how soft and warm they'd been and begged his magic to fashion a way to feel them again. "Isabella has a list of herbs for us to purchase from town. She says the desert merchant should have arrived by now. We'll go as soon as you've eaten and dressed."

"Thank you," Nezael whispered and like all mornings, Yorick took his leave silently.

Nezael furiously wiped his eyes, willing back the

tears gathering for months at the loss of something once so profound, and focused on his breakfast. Cinnamon spiced porridge with a slice of bread baked with a cinnamon swirl. No icing, but Nezael found himself more than fine with that. Nezael breathed in the aroma, knowing the cinnamon and sweetness was Yorick's own touch to show he cared, and ate.

He couldn't change what happened. Day by day, the hurt faded. One day, it'd simply be and he and Yorick would continue to be whatever they were now. Warm or cold to one another, it didn't matter. Their lives were entwined forevermore.

~

WARMTH STRETCHED ACROSS THE LAND, THE SUN ABOVE bright. Dew glistened beneath it so early in the morning. Everything was honestly so vibrant and cheerful, it soured Nezael's mood even more. The warmth dictated a lack of a cloak for Nezael, and he'd dressed simply like any other traveler with a thin billowing linen shirt cut low with light breeches Lord Carrow had given him recently. Too normal of an outfit for a necromancer; Nezael would rather be in his magic armor.

Yorick, meanwhile, had learned very quickly how to wrap a scarf around his skull to hide his skeletal visage. Unfortunately, with his height, he turned a lot of heads, and Nezael had to learn a glamouring spell to make people not notice him so often. He'd never needed it for Agatha or Isabella so it was just one more thing to learn.

The markets in town were crowded in the summer, the thrum of bodies bustling past one another to lighten their coin purses. Many were locals, but also travelers passing by the area. It was also in such crowds, people began to notice Nezael and tried to engage with him more than they ever had before. He never bothered to respond; he had herbs to get and then he'd return to the safety of the drafty tower that was home. No matter how often there was the soft press of fingers against his arm to get his attention, smiles when Nezael looked at them, or the voices flirting with him to see if he cared, he wasn't going to be tempted.

When Nezael expressed his concerns with the new-found attention, Carrow simply told him he'd ceased glamouring Nezael to go by unnoticed. Damning as it was to be enchanted and not even know it, Carrow also told him to use the attention to his advantage. Bring un-suspecting people to the tower to have more skeleton fodder.

"It worked once, after all," Carrow had said with such a self-serving smile, Nezael wanted to scream. He'd held it in then, however, and simply bowed.

Carrow acted like Yorick was on purpose. Yet he *knew* he wasn't, but it was all part of the punishment. Even more, that Carrow believed Nezael wanted to draw others into his bed only to pull them apart like they were nothing made him sick. Nezael wanted none of that. He'd rather find a poor body abandoned in the woods and make a skeleton from that than anyone he tricked, no matter how much weaker the skeleton would be.

In response to the newfound attention in town, all Nezael could do was smile, whisper a platitude that meant nothing, and leave before anyone thought to grow bolder. Yorick sometimes stepped in, but that would risk his glamour, so he and Nezael agreed he'd only do so if someone turned to anger after a rejection. Seldom did it happen, but Nezael hated having to deal with the touches at all, knowing Yorick was right there beside him having to endure watching it the same.

The herbs today came from an older woman dressed in colorful clothes. She arrived only in the summertime and was always sought after. Herbs grown in the desert were rare in these parts and she happily parted with her rarities for sufficient coin.

These herbs were essential to keeping them safe. Would-be heroes, thieves, and spies sought their tower for nefarious means and Carrow used a potion derived from these herbs and others to suss out enemies before he tore them apart. Even mercenaries he'd hired weren't spared; one thought against anyone in the tower and that'd be that. Sometimes, they deserved it too.

And, once more, Nezael found himself so deep in his head thinking of everything and nothing to detach himself from reality, he'd blanked out the purchasing and the walk away from the crowds. It was only when he felt the wood of a bridge beneath his feet did he jolt back. He slowed and considered the holly still wrapped around the posts. Traces of his magic bloomed still, keeping the holly alive. A spell he'd never tell Carrow of.

"Nezael?" Yorick whispered his name so soothingly, Nezael shivered.

"It's fine," Nezael insisted and continued.

"Bellamy said all our lord's experiments stay deep in the forest," Yorick said as he walked in stride beside Nezael. "But... thank you for keeping the charms going.

The town may never know, but it means a lot to me."

Nezael nodded, but did not smile. It was through no act of altruism; simply self-serving. A way to assuage the guilt eating him up from the inside. One day, Carrow *would* come for the bones in town and no one—no charms, no magic spell, not even Nezael—could stop him. Nezael buried the feeling, let the guilt burn him until he was nothing inside. It was easier that way.

The walk back was bereft of any meaningful conversation. Nezael preferred it, especially now. He was sure he and Yorick had plenty to say to each other, but neither wanted to parse the thoughts into words. What was done was done. Easier to bury it like everything else.

The afternoon sun was as bright as the morning had been, making the green leaves glitter when the wind rustled through them. There were a few other travelers on the road, but their pace was quick while Nezael kept his and Yorick's slow. They came to the path leading into the wards too soon for Nezael's liking, and like always, Nezael feigned a break to drink some water.

Yorick's fingers grazed Nezael's side and he paused.

"Someone's been following us," Yorick said, his words almost silent if not for the magic linking them together.

Nezael gulped down some water and made a show of dousing his head as though to cool off to give himself a reason to turn. A young man flinched out of sight too quick for Nezael to see much of him. Most people interested in propositioning Nezael directly did sometimes follow him away from the crowd because of their own shyness, but not once did they jump to hide behind

a tree when Nezael noticed them. Muggers would have
already charged Nezael, thinking him vulnerable, only to
be met with a tall skeleton's fist.

This one likely wanted something else, but Nezael
didn't want to bother.

"He's skittish," Nezael whispered. "Once we're
through the ward, we'll lose him and he'll lose us."

It was how Nezael lost insistent pursuers who followed him from town. Though he'd once loved when
Yorick teased him about being a nymph, he now hated it
because it was how many saw him now. A flighty nymph
with a coy smile who disappeared into the woods. And, if
Carrow commanded it, Yorick or Bellamy would be
ordered to kill any stray person lost in the woods from
trying to follow Nezael. Then the body would become
bones in a pile to make something new, bereft of all soul
and thought. A mindless soldier ready to one day burn
the land.

Nezael wouldn't mention this poor soul to Carrow.

The ward accepted them through, obscuring the
woods behind the veil of magic, and Nezael breathed out.
A headache bloomed behind his eyes, drawing deep
from his overall exhaustion, but he forged on instead of
the summertime nap he would have partaken in if it'd
been the year before. Lord Carrow would want his
assistance after last night. Nezael already smelled the
blood on the air wafting from the tower.

He'd wanted to forget the poor soul his lord had
invited to stay the night, but now Nezael had to
acknowledge the man was there. Bones and all.

The tower greeted Nezael as it always did, its doors

thrown open wide today to usher in the breeze, but unlike the sundrenched paths before, there was only darkness pervading just inside. Bellamy waited for him at the doorway. His friendly demeanor had returned, but Nezael knew differently now. It had always been a rouse, hiding the sad man underneath it all. It buried Bellamy's own guilt and continued to do so.

"Ah, there you two are." Bellamy waved Yorick over and Nezael let him go with the bag of herbs across his shoulder. "I see you were able to get all what Izzy needed." Bellamy nodded, checking the bag, and left it with Yorick. "I am to show Yorick"—he said the name so much softer than anyone else's, like he was admitting his own guilt in Yorick's creation—"our summer defenses. He will be in charge of their upkeep."

Anything to keep Yorick away from Nezael. Honestly, Carrow could do whatever he wanted to Yorick and Nezael would have to watch in horror. As Yorick learned early on, he went without a fuss. No broken bones like he'd endured the first time he'd hesitated listening to Carrow's orders. Nezael had healed the bones in secret, whispering apology after apology in the dark and Yorick had tended to Nezael the same when their lord found out.

Nezael walked alone into the thoroughfare and followed Carrow's magic tugging him softly. The great hall was lit in soft candlelight as the first storm clouds of summer began to hide the cheerful sun. Soon, rain would pelt the windows, ghosting another chill through the drafty hallways, but for now, an appropriate gloom settled over the room.

There was a body yet again upon the plinth. Another one wrapped in bloodied linen floated, suspended in place as though waiting its turn patiently beside his lord.

Carrow hadn't changed a bit since waking. Ever invigorated from his sleep over the winter, the man had returned to necromancy with a certain glee and sought Nezael's help far more often than he had before like Nezael truly was ready for all the truths and lies necromancy brought.

Today, like all days dealing with a cadaver, Carrow's hands and arms were stained with blood as he extracted everything useful from within. He gleefully ripped out the innards and organs because it was *his* body to do with what he wanted. Some fascination putting those who thought Carrow simply an eccentric sorcerer in their place. Many mercenaries faced that fate.

Nezael avoided the smile Carrow gave him as he approached and peered over the body instead. This was the mercenary who had dined with them to talk plans. Nezael didn't know what those plans were. When he came in to serve them wine and food, they had already moved on. The mercenary, upon seeing Nezael, decided instead to talk about what he'd do to Nezael if he could. Though Nezael's body had burned with embarrassment hearing such things said aloud, Carrow simply urged the man on, amused, and eventually invited the man to stay the night with Nezael.

Despite all the man's big words, his touch had been featherlight like he was afraid to do all the things he'd said. Bravado to mask his uneasiness with Carrow, Nezael supposed. Or he was spurred on to say such things because it amused his lord. Whatever the case, the man had quickly drunk the wine Nezael brought for him. Maybe he'd been hoping to steel his resolve. All the wine did, however, was put him to sleep and then stopped his heart.

Sleep was a mercy. The potion could be done without it and Carrow preferred it that way to not be wasteful; dead was dead, whether it was painless or not. Nezael, however, refused to serve it without the sleeping draught. Last night, he'd left the man slumbering happily in the guest room. Sometime later, the man had died.

Guilt gnawed at Nezael's stomach and he glanced at the body suspended in the air. Didn't know that one, at least. Perhaps a spy or some would-be hero catching wind of rumors Carrow cared naught to squash. Let the bodies come, he insisted. He'd put them to use.

"Oh, my little blossom," Carrow murmured. "Why so dour?" He ushered Nezael closer with a bloodied hand. "You've been so cold to me lately. Did you not have fun last night?"

"It was a simple night," Nezael said. Carrow knew what hadn't happened. He knew everything Nezael did in the guestroom with all their invited guests over the months. The mirror was enchanted. Nezael had gone through great pains to learn if his own was enchanted and thankfully, it was not. He hoped it stayed that way.

Carrow smiled nonetheless and shrugged. "Men are often so full of their own words to hide a lack of action." He indicated the body before them. "I've muddied his memories enough, he won't remember the night, but he'll keep his wonderful talent for organization once we raise him. One more step toward a new life."

A fleeting promise, but Nezael nodded.

"Come and help me."

Nezael paused and glanced at himself. "I should change, then."

"Perish the thought, my blossom." Carrow's hand was quick as it caught Nezael's arm. Fingers tight, he pulled Nezael in front of him. From behind, Carrow pressed his bloodied hands against Nezael's shirt. "We have many shirts such as this." Carrow dragged the shirt downward, letting his nails rake across Nezael's flesh, and Nezael let him. It was easier that way. His lord pressed a kiss to Nezael's exposed neck. "Let me see this one ravaged. You are so incredibly stunning feral and blood-ied and I will have it to memorize."

All Nezael could do was follow his lord's motion while locking his thoughts away so nothing mattered. Not the blood between his fingers. Not the red blooming across his shirt so he may never wear it again. Not the way his lord watched him, hungry like a beast waiting to devour him whole.

~

BY THE TIME NEZAEL WASHED OFF THE BLOOD, SCRUBBED his skin so raw, his own blood joined it in the heat of the bath, his body was exhausted, aching, and he forgot all about his adventures into town. He collapsed into bed, hair still damp, and tried to sleep it all away. Try to dream of the kisses that never came. He was starkly aware of its absence in the dark and wondered if he'd even slept. Morning came veiled by rain and soft thunder in the distance.

And with Yorick's hand on his shoulder.

Nezael jolted, the touch of skin gone too soon and replaced with the fabric wrapped around his skeletal fingers.

"Nezael," Yorick whispered, his hollow voice further grounding Nezael in the reality of what he'd done to Yorick. What was more alarming was that Yorick had ceased coming into Nezael's room until he was fully awake at Carrow's insistence. Yet here he was now.

"Get dressed." Yorick dropped Nezael's necromancer robes onto his lap. "Please."

"What's wrong?" Nezael swung his legs over the side of the bed. "Did something happen?"

"I found a body in the cellarage." Yorick paused. "I... I recognize him from yesterday."

Nezael dressed as quickly as he could with Yorick's help to fashion the golden spine against his back for his magic armor. Its warmth fluttered across him, making him feel light, and they hurried down to the cellarage.

Full of dusty cobwebs, items which had long since lost their purpose, and food canned and preserved alongside Carrow's casks of wine was indeed a body. A young man. The wards had gotten him, leaving his body there preserved for their taking, but still very dead. Bright blue eyes without the luster of life behind them. Thick blonde hair tumbled to one side and his pale skin was covered in freckles. He was slender, all soft angles, and reminded Nezael of himself. He wore a simple traveling tunic which hid glistening knives within. Breeches held nothing more than a bag of what he'd already managed to grab. He had no shoes to speak of, but Nezael wondered if he'd taken them off to sneak around without them.

Regardless, he'd made it here. Inside. Through the exterior wards only to be trounced by the internal ones.

"He was the young man who followed us out of town," Yorick whispered.

Oh. Nezael's skin washed cold with the realization. It didn't quite answer the how, but Nezael hated himself all the more. If he'd let Yorick scare the man away, or even confronted him on his own, he could have stopped a senseless death. Nezael squeezed his eyes shut to push back the headache threatening to claw across his scalp. How many deaths was he up to now? It did him no good to count, yet he tried and quickly lost the number.

Yorick was kneeling beside him, skeletal hand pressed to the small of his back to keep him balanced. He needed it. So he could think. Decide what he wanted to do with the man. A proper burial? Or take him into their fold? What would he have wanted? What did Nezael even want?

Too many questions. Nezael wanted to go back to a dark room and shut it all out.

Until he heard footsteps echoing down the stairs. Yorick's arm slid away and he stood, acting like the bodyguard he should have been and not the friend he was. Carrow came down with Bellamy at his heels and they slowed upon seeing Nezael kneeling on the floor. His expression lifted into delight once he sighted the dead young man.

"Oh," he said. "I see Bellamy is correct. We've a new friend."

"I don't know how he got so far," Nezael said.

The delight melted into concern, stopping Carrow in his tracks. He hummed thoughtfully before stepping beside Nezael. "I suppose you will simply have to replace all our wards. Your distraction this winter made them woefully weak, my blossom." One hand gently reached out and drew itself through Nezael's hair.

"Yes, my lord," Nezael whispered, knowing any other response would dig his lord's fingers into his scalp.

"But, for now, we have a new friend." Carrow attempted to swoop down to gather the young man, but Nezael blocked him with an arm. Anger flashed in Carrow's eyes, but Nezael didn't draw back.

"He is not yours," Nezael said slowly. "He's mine."

Without even looking, Nezael felt Yorick stiffen behind him. The subtle click of his bones and the softest gasp. Carrow raised his eyebrows.

"Oh, is he, my blossom?" He slid his gaze to Yorick, a mean smirk jutting across his lips, and once more, he drew his fingers through Nezael's hair. Softer this time. "What makes you so sure?"

"Our skeletons of late have had more of my magic than yours," Nezael said quietly. Carrow's eyes narrowed. Nezael had noticed it from the first one after Yorick, but he'd been unsure about asking why. "Yet you always have control over them. If I am to be your necromancer, I feel I should have more of my own. I can do this myself. All of it. Let me prove it."

Genuine surprise crossed his lord's face before it settled into a haughty smile. He fully expected Nezael to fail. Maybe he would. "Raising someone you hardly even know is quite different. And this one, you don't even have the pleasure of fucking beforehand." His fingers drew downward along Nezael's jaw before he tipped Nezael's chin upward to look at him. "But, if you truly seek to ravage yourself attempting the feat on your own, he's all yours."

Before Carrow stood, he pressed his lips to Nezael's. He knew what he was doing. He knew Yorick was there watching him. The kiss lingered longer than Nezael wanted it to and then all at once, Carrow had drawn himself to his full height and left. Bellamy lingered, words there in his skeletal visage until Carrow sharply called his name from above. He left as well, leaving Nezael alone with Yorick and the poor dead man.

A burning sensation raced through Nezael's body knowing how intently Yorick was watching him.

"Nezael..."

The spell to make objects float was simple. Bodies were decidedly less simple than objects, but Nezael drew the magic threads around the body the same anyway. They became soft glimmers weaved together as a kind of burial shroud. Once Nezael was sure it'd be steady, he drew the threads upward with him as he stood. The body floated off the ground, suspended on magic alone.

"Nezael: look at me," Yorick said louder.

And Nezael couldn't. Not until Yorick gripped his chin and forced him to. There was nothing to see there. A skull stared back at him, but Nezael felt the heat of his glare regardless.

"You can't be serious," he whispered. "You'll trap him here with you for the misfortune of following us?

Just to prove you can? Does he truly deserve that fate?"

Had Yorick truly deserved his fate was the question Nezael asked every day. The one hidden behind this one now as the regret pulled Yorick's voice taut.

"Better me than our lord," Nezael said, words heavy on his tongue. "I know what I'm doing."

"Do you? Truly?" The anger lashed out and Nezael flinched. "Forcing him—"

"I did *not* force you," Nezael growled and Yorick stilled. "I gave you the only choice I could give. Die or stay with me. I will give him the same. If you now think you can do better elsewhere, then go. My magic is not so weak you'll fall apart without me."

Nezael wanted to take back the words as soon as he'd said them. They were unfair. Yorick would be struck down by would-be heroes without a thought, no matter how kind he might have been. Beyond that, the words dredged up thoughts and feelings he'd buried over the spring to make this work. Once more, Carrow's machinations attempted to push them apart. Except this time, it was evident the hurt was still there. Bleeding over. Festering unseen for the both of them.

"You can come with me," Yorick tried, his voice so small and quiet.

"There's nothing out there for a necromancer such as me," Nezael whispered and looked away. What would Carrow do if he tried to run now? What would happen to the skeletons here he'd come to adore as though they were his own? Even the town would not be spared should Nezael attempt escape. Carrow knew how soft Nezael was and he'd willingly use it against him. Like he already had. "I am Lord Carrow's apprentice and that is all I'll ever be."

It hurt to say it so succinctly, but Nezael wouldn't have anywhere to go. As soon as someone learned he was a necromancer, he'd be executed on the spot and he wasn't quite quick enough with magic like Carrow to avoid death completely.

Yorick stared at him, finally silent, and walked away.

It was deserved. All the regret. The anger. The sadness. It burned inside Nezael through the entire trek back to the ritual room and threatened to overrun every time he had to catch the body, his attention too frayed to keep the spell tight like it should have been. Once inside the ritual room, Nezael buried the feelings the best he could so he could be the necromancer his lord wished him to be.

The clothes came off with a spell as Nezael gathered the instruments from Carrow's workshop (and Carrow's magic gleefully showed him which tools to use). Isabella helped him gather the correct herbs from her stores, but she gave him no advice. No soft words. Nezael didn't want them. Not anymore.

Before the first incision, before Nezael took anything hidden beneath the skin, he paused and stared at the freckled young man lying there on the plinth. An undeserved fate befalling him for nothing more than being curious.

"Hello," Nezael whispered, drawing his fingers softly along his cold cheek. "I know not if you can hear me as you are, but... what do you want?" He felt silly asking it aloud, but he owed the young man that much.

After a silent moment, the ghost of a touch fluttered across his hands in response. Acknowledgement *something* was there. Nezael smiled softly.

"I can let you go, if you so wish. But, if you are not tired of living, I can invite you back into the body you once called home. It will be... different. All you need to do is tell me."

The words Nezael should have asked Yorick, but by the time he even knew what was going on, Yorick had already been carved open. Still, Nezael wished he'd asked, even if he wasn't sure Yorick would have said no. Not the way his soul had wrapped around him like the lover he'd been as Nezael rested beside his skeleton. Not how quickly his soul came when all the magic set itself against the bones. Yorick had risen so easily, saying no had never crossed the man's mind.

Even if he now regretted it.

This soul, the one Nezael should have been focusing on, was shy and soft. He hadn't left his body. The softest touch trailed up Nezael's arm and a breath ghosted against his ear.

"*My name is Cassius,*" the voice whispered and Nezael repeated the name to himself. "*And I am not yet through with this world.*"

"Then I shall begin," Nezael murmured. "And... I'm sorry."

By himself with none of Carrow's guidance or even a skeleton to help, the process took so long with many back-and-forths between the plinth and the spell book he'd gone to gather from the library. In that time, the storm passed, leaving an afternoon sun making the room glow as Nezael worked. The skin came off easily now. The heart went down better, its blood bright red against Nezael's fingers. Against Cassius' pale freckled skin. On and on the ritual went until the organs were harvested, the waste magically folded into the tower to augment what little remained of the wards, and Nezael finally mixed his blood with Cassius' for the life blossom heart.

Cassius' skeleton was much slighter than Yorick's was. Not the hulking bodyguard Yorick had become, then. Cassius would be something else entirely. Perhaps a spy to work quick through the night.

Nezael cleaned his hands and face with a basin of cold water he'd conjured into the room. He had no reason to look so feral if his lord was not there to see it. The water ran red in mere moments and Nezael left it be. Magic was continuing to coalesce around the skeleton, the gossamer shroud sealing it in as the soul touched what it had become. It could still fail. If Cassius rejected seeing his skeleton laid so bare, he would simply pass on and they'd have bones to use for something else.

Either way, Carrow would win.

The door opened. Air blew through the room, rustling the gossamer shroud. Nezael whipped around to look, expecting Carrow's intrusion, but it was Yorick.

Relief washed through Nezael first; Yorick hadn't up and left. But then devastation followed; he'd given Yorick the only out he could give him and yet the man stayed to be tortured day in and day out in a life he did not want in the least. Nezael's eyes burned with tears as Yorick came up to him silently.

"Yorick—"

"Nezael," Yorick murmured his name so softly, Nezael hesitated. He had his hands clasped together and after a moment longer, he held out a small flower from within. Yellow, it was bright and vibrant in the room growing cold and dim. "Do not apologize. I am being difficult with you the more time moves on."

Nezael took the flower and realized what it was from. A blossom of the vistarium herbs he'd gone searching for what felt like years ago and only to find Yorick instead.

"I should tell you my plans, all of them," Nezael whispered. "I want no secrets between us."

"And I know you will share them." Yorick cupped Nezael's face and tilted him to look up. At eye sockets once holding his blue eyes. At a handsome face still handsome even as a skull with no skin or smile to speak of. "I want to stay with you, Nezael. You are right. I did choose. And I think, even if asked to choose again, I would choose the same. I willingly gave you my heart, after all. We will make this work." His voice drew quieter. "Not like before, but I meant what I said."

Nezael touched Yorick's hand against his face. It felt warm, somehow like it had before during sleepy days in Yorick's cabin.

"I am yours, forevermore." Yorick bent lower and Nezael felt lips kiss his own. Magic had listened to his plea and fashioned itself into something tangible. All to remind him of what he'd lost. It would go no further than a soft kiss. The memory would fade, continue to do so as the days wore on, and the magic would cease trying.

"I love you, Yorick," Nezael whispered it so quietly, afraid Carrow would hear otherwise. He kissed Yorick's jaw, and forced the magic to part so all he felt was the skull against his lips. This was his Yorick now and he'd love him the same.

With a nod, Yorick withdrew, but he said no more as he walked out, leaving Nezael with the golden flower.

Nezael faced Cassius. The magic around him felt indignant now and Nezael chuckled. "I am sorry to have ignored you so, my dear Cassius. But what of you getting jealous? You hardly even know me." He gently laid himself beside the skeleton as he'd done to Yorick upon the same plinth. He tucked the yellow blossom into Cassius' ribcage, hoping to keep it safe within Cassius' new heart. "Perhaps you and I could be friends?"

Because no matter what Cassius wanted, Nezael had already given his heart away. Even Carrow would come to understand that one day. To be Lord Carrow's apprentice—his necromancer—Nezael preferred to be heartless anyway. It made it all easier.

Although, maybe one day, he'd find his heart whole again with the man he'd given it to.

~

ABOUT THE AUTHOR

S. Jean (she/they) is a queer sci-fi & fantasy author writing whatever strikes their fancy at any given moment. When not writing or dreaming of what to write, they can be found dabbling in game dev and drawing!

For more information,
visit: https://sjean.carrd.co/